"It's No Secret That You Were Enjoying What We Were Doing As Much As I Was."

He shot her a swift look that contained no small element of surprise. "You're right," he admitted. "I was. But you're . . . well, not the sort of girl I'd care to inveigle into an affair."

"What kind of girl—no, woman—do you think I am?"

"The nice, decent kind—as dangerous as they come. Not to mention passionate and desirable. If you want the truth, I'm sorry I can't take advantage of the latter qualities."

SUZANNE CAREY

is a reporter by training but a romance writer by choice. She likes to research her stories carefully and write about the places and people she knows best. For this reason, her books have a real-life quality that intrigues readers as much as it touches their hearts.

Dear Reader:

SILHOUETTE DESIRE is an exciting new line of contemporary romances from Silhouette Books. During the past year, many Silhouette readers have written in telling us what other types of stories they'd like to read from Silhouette, and we've kept these comments and suggestions in mind in developing SILHOUETTE DESIRE.

DESIREs feature all of the elements you like to see in a romance, plus a more sensual, provocative story. So if you want to experience all the excitement, passion and joy of falling in love, then SILHOUETTE DESIRE is for you.

Karen Solem
Editor-in-Chief
Silhouette Books

SUZANNE CAREY
Angel in His Arms

Silhouette Desire
Published by Silhouette Books New York
America's Publisher of Contemporary Romance

SILHOUETTE BOOKS
300 E. 42nd St., New York, N.Y. 10017

Copyright © 1985 by Suzanne Carey

Distributed by Pocket Books

All rights reserved, including the right to reproduce
this book or portions thereof in any form whatsoever.
For information address Silhouette Books,
300 E. 42nd St., New York, N.Y. 10017

ISBN: 0-373-05206-5

First Silhouette Books printing May, 1985

10 9 8 7 6 5 4 3 2 1

All of the characters in this book are fictitious. Any resemblance to actual persons, living or dead, is purely coincidental.

SILHOUETTE, SILHOUETTE DESIRE and
colophon are registered trademarks of the publisher.

America's Publisher of Contemporary Romance

Printed in the U.S.A.

Books by Suzanne Carey

Silhouette Desire

For my beautiful daughter Amy

Angel
in His Arms

1

At last she had the key, though she was reluctant now to use it. Almost apprehensively, she sat at her father's battered old desk, listening to the quiet and considering what she might find.

By now, everyone who had crowded into the four-room frame house beside Bayou Black after the funeral had gone. Even their closest neighbors, Jim and Leonie Boudreaux, had departed, after repeated assurances from Annie that she would be fine there alone.

My closest neighbors, she corrected, letting the fact of her father's death sink in as far as it could. Yet try as she would to face them, the events of the past week just didn't seem real. Surely at any moment stocky, taciturn Ned Duprez would be tying up his boat at the little dock outside. He would be pulling off his boots and leaving them on the linoleum beside the stove in the kitchen,

11

whistling faintly as he lifted the lid on whatever she was cooking for supper.

There wouldn't have been much dinner-table conversation—just an offhand mention of how many nutria Ned had caught that day, what had happened at her job as a music teacher in the Terrebonne Parish schools. Doubtless her father would have shrugged and voiced a complaint or two about the oil companies that dominated the marsh these days, making a trapper's living more difficult to earn.

Yet the two of them had been close, united by a deep bond of affection even if Ned had never really understood the daughter who'd been left behind for him to raise.

Now she was alone for the first time in her life— single, though her father had hoped she would marry a local man and settle down; sole resident of the house where it seemed she had lived forever except during her college days in Lafayette.

For the first time, she lacked the boundaries her father's presence had set in her life. No longer could she postpone her dreams with the excuse that she couldn't hurt him by following in her mother's footsteps. No longer was there any reason not to face the past—or delay sifting through Ned's secret cache of memories.

She was fairly certain that's what the single, shallow drawer of his desk contained: mementos of Solange Trosclair Duprez, the wife he'd refused to talk about and the mother Annie had never known.

With a little tremor of anticipation, she fitted the key into the lock and turned it. He must have guessed I would want some answers, she thought. She'd been told very little of the story, after all. Just that Solange had run away from Carteret, her family's River Road plantation, to marry an uneducated trapper-fisherman, then bolted a second time to pursue a brief fling as a jazz singer in New Orleans before her untimely death.

There had been an unspoken assumption, fed by Ned's tight-lipped silence, that Solange had been a wayward woman who had preferred the company of many men to that of one devoted husband, a woman who had left her child without a backward glance.

Despite his mute condemnation, Annie admitted more to curiosity about her mother than anger or a sense of betrayal. Now, as the desk drawer yielded up its secrets, her wide gray gaze settled first on a poorly exposed black-and-white snapshot. Its subject was a slim, sweet-faced girl dressed in shapeless cotton. Standing with one oxford-clad foot poised on a cypress knee, she had her arms entwined about a chubby toddler. Her fragile, almost luminous quality tugged at the heart.

It was the first picture of Solange that Annie had ever seen. *My mother,* Annie thought with a little shiver of recognition. *And me.* Probably Ned had taken them out on Lake Hatch in the boat one Sunday afternoon and snapped the photo near his trapping shack. It was a spot Annie in later years had come to love.

Gooseflesh stood out on her skin as she stared at this small vignette from the past; incredibly, she was able to see herself not just in the child, but in the woman. For there was no denying it—Solange Duprez had been the author of Annie's brilliant yet hesitant smile, her slender, long-legged grace. Even the shyness that had always plagued her was discernable in her mother's countenance.

Ned had let it slip once, when whiskey had loosened his tongue, that it was Solange's charming reticence that had attracted him most when she had turned up as an outsider at the annual Chauvin festival and agreed to dance with him.

I must have been all of two years old when this picture was taken, Annie conjectured with a lump in her throat, noting her own blond halo of baby curls. Her hair had since darkened to an almost light brown color. In the photo, Solange's hair was as light as her child's. Doubtless she had bleached it for effect—perhaps in anticipation of the career that would take her out of their lives forever.

Annie's hand shook a little as she laid the snapshot aside. In its place she picked up an eighteen-year-old newspaper clipping, yellowing and fragile. According to the story, a brief review from the *New Orleans Times-Picayune,* her mother had been a modest success, attracting a crowd of regulars and tourists to a Bourbon Street club called the Red Door. The writer had remarked on her air of innocence, calling it a refreshingly rare commodity on the city scene.

She could only guess what her father's reaction must have been to that. How ironic it must have seemed to him that men in the smoky little cabaret had viewed Solange not as a scarlet woman but as an angel.

Caught by warring emotions, Annie removed several pieces of sheet music from the drawer, scores for songs that had been popular forty or fifty years before. The titles were all swing band favorites—exactly the sort of music Annie had sung professionally for a brief period and come to love. I don't believe it, she thought. It's as if I'd inherited her taste along with the color of her eyes. These songs were old even when she was at the height of her career.

A moment later, she was catching her breath anew.

There beneath the sheet music, held together by a rubber band and stuffed inside a torn envelope, was a packet of bank drafts. They had been drawn on a New Orleans bank in the early years of Annie's childhood, but never cashed. Had Solange sent money for her support, then? she wondered. Money Ned in his anger and pride had disdained to use?

She could think of no other explanation. The drafts, made out to Ned with Solange as payer, totaled nearly a thousand dollars—no small piece of change to a struggling young singer so long ago. Apparently Solange had felt some concern after all for the blond toddler she'd held in her arms.

Suddenly it was as if a dam had broken. Annie couldn't stem the tears that spilled down her cheeks; they seemed to come from some deep, untouched part of herself. All her life she had loved Ned Duprez, the reserved father who had indulged in his funny stories and Cajun folk songs only when he'd had too much liquor in him, but who had always been there to bandage skinned knees and quiet her small-girl fears.

Yet she felt something like the beginnings of love, too, for the unknown girl-woman in the photograph. Along with the love was an uncomfortable feeling of disloyalty to her father. Still, she was filled with a strong and undeniable longing to know the truth—both about Solange and about herself.

In the past, like Ned, she had kept her own counsel. Not once had she hinted at any desire to be a singer, though her voice coach at the university had been lavish with praise and she'd received favorable notices for her brief stint in a Lafayette bar. Instead, she had sublimated her gift in teaching. Her father had approved of the choice, though he'd regarded it as temporary, something to tide her over until she married and became the mother of his grandchildren.

He'd never been able to understand why she didn't fall in love with one of the serious-minded young mechanics and netmakers and fishermen who escorted her to Saturday night dances. Meanwhile, the desire to leave Houma and try for a singing career had continued to burn in Annie like a flame.

Dabbing at her eyes, she regarded the snapshot again. I wish I could have cared for one of the men he favored, she thought. Things might have been easier that way. But I'm more like Solange than he ever guessed. I want to sweep an audience up in a world of my own creation, make people feel music as I do so that they go away uplifted and changed. If I'm ever to have a man of my own, he'll have to understand that, not try to put me in a box and keep me there.

At the same time, her mother's example had made her wary. If she made it as a singer, she believed, there wouldn't be any room in her life for a family. I won't ever do what *she* did, Annie vowed—leave a husband and child hostages to fortune.

Only a few items remained in the drawer: a plain gold wedding ring large enough to fit her father's finger, and two envelopes that were empty of the letters they'd once contained. One of them, addressed to Annie's father, gave as a return address a New Orleans boardinghouse. The other had been sent to Herve Trosclair in Vacherie, Annie's maternal grandfather. Apparently it had been returned unopened.

As clues, they offered scant information. Yet by the time she had looked quietly at her mother's picture once more and put the small collection of mementos back in their resting place, she had made up her mind. If

Luray Burns, the music teacher who had retired several years ago, could be prevailed upon to replace her, she would request a leave of absence for the remainder of the school year. Closing up the house, she would take her modest savings, plus the bank drafts if they could still be cashed, and set out on a journey of discovery.

Later, as she turned out the light, she rehearsed her plan. She would go first to Vacherie and confront her Trosclair relatives, demand to be told what they knew. Then she would head into New Orleans, look for a singing job, and seek out what traces of her mother she could find.

But neither Solange's past nor Annie's own prospects claimed her final waking thoughts that night. Instead, loneliness intruded, and as she fell into sleep she found herself dreaming of a dark and knowing stranger, one who moved at ease in the glamorous world she hoped to make her own.

A week later, Annie was riding north toward Vacherie in Joe Guidry's ice truck, her mother's photo and the few tattered sheets of music Ned had saved tucked in her suitcase. Her father's pickup had been totally demolished in the accident following his heart attack, and she had decided not to replace it in order to save as much money as she could.

Cashing the bank drafts hadn't been easy. Uncertain what to do, the teller had called for her supervisor, who in turn had summoned the bank manager. There had been a long-distance call to her mother's former bank in New Orleans. But finally they had counted out the money, and she had added it to her modest store.

I'm going to miss Houma and the swamp and even my students, she thought now, looking out at the neat bottomland farms that lined the highway, meanwhile murmuring appropriate responses to Joe Guidry's steady stream of conversation. But I couldn't stay there forever. I have to give myself this chance.

She fell silent, her heart beating a little faster, as they came into Vacherie, an ordinary enough small town with ranch-style houses and banks and a post office lining the highway. Route 20 dead-ended at the river levee, and the truck driver, an old friend of her father's, turned west toward Carteret.

Despite the fact that she had lived only forty miles or so from the place where her mother had been raised, Annie hadn't seen it before, avoiding it perhaps out of a sense of loyalty to her father. Now that she was actually approaching, she still wasn't sure she'd been right to come. The Trosclairs might not welcome her, after all, might not even open their door to someone claiming kinship to Solange Duprez.

Yet though her stomach seemed tied into little knots, she was overwhelmed with curiosity. Hungrily her gaze drank in every aspect of the rural scene—cows grazing placidly on the grassy slope of levee that blocked any view of the river, flat fields of sugar cane, plantation houses hidden among the trees.

"This is Carteret," Joe announced, pulling into a gravel drive shaded by only a scattering of oaks. "I came up here with Ned to get your mother's things maybe twenty-seven years ago."

Annie stared, surprised to learn that someone outside the family had been privy to memories she'd never shared. But all her real attention was for the Trosclair home. It was more Creole farmhouse than antebellum mansion, she saw, a throwback to the French settlement of the area before the days of the sugar barons. A

18

broad exterior staircase rose above the lower story to an overhanging wooden gallery defined by narrow posts and a low railing. The massive, steeply pitched roof was of tin, rusting a little and adorned with two dormers and a pair of chimneys. But even though the house needed paint, and the shrubbery around it had received only the most perfunctory care, Carteret exemplified balance and grace, an airy comfort suited to the warm, damp climate.

"Shall I drive up to the door?" Joe asked, watching her with quiet concern. "I ain't in any hurry. If you want, I can wait."

"No, thanks, Joe. I really appreciate the ride. But you understand, don't you? I . . . won't be going back to Houma today."

With the palms of her hands perspiring a little, she got out and accepted her single suitcase. Already she had seen a curtain at one of the windows lift a little and then fall back into place.

For one desolate moment she watched the cloud of white dust thrown up by Joe's truck as he backed out of the drive and returned toward Vacherie to make his deliveries. Then, as she turned back toward the house, the front door opened. "Afternoon," a thin, dark, middle-aged man greeted her doubtfully.

Annie swallowed. "Mr. Trosclair?"

He nodded.

"I'm Annie Duprez, Solange's daughter."

Annie would never be exactly sure how she came to be in Carteret's shuttered parlor with her cousin Zenon Trosclair. Only one thing was certain: this dark, sallow man was even more ill at ease than she.

Her voice a little unsteady in her own ears, Annie

answered his few brief questions, then listened quietly while he explained that her grandfather, Herve Trosclair, had died some ten years before. "My father, Alphonse, your . . . uh, mother's brother, is the owner now," he said. "My sister Addie and I live here with him. I manage the Vacherie branch of the Plantation Bank and Trust." He paused. "May I ask . . . why you came here now, after all these years?"

To her surprise, she found she didn't want to explain about Ned's bitterness and his secret drawer, or to be as demanding as she'd planned. "My father died recently," she said. "I'm on my way to New Orleans. While I'm there, I want to trace my mother's background. I was hoping her family could help."

Zenon Trosclair was silent a moment. Watching him, Annie thought he must be a very cautious and private man. "Her name hasn't been mentioned here willingly since the day she left," he admitted finally. "I'm not sure Papa would thank me for askin' you in here now. Still . . ." He hesitated. "I can understand your desire to find out what happened. Personally, I don't remember her well. You see, I was just a boy when she left. But . . . after she died . . . the owner of the boardin' house where she lived sent us her belongin's. They're still upstairs in the attic. I don't see why I can't give them to you."

Annie followed her cousin up a dark, narrow stairway. But Solange's pasteboard suitcase, worn and tied with a length of rope where one of the fasteners had broken, contained only a few possessions: a baby picture of Annie; more sheet music, mostly scores for the World War II era jazz tunes that had been her specialty; and some clothing in the style of the early sixties, which ironically had become fashionable again. Most of her clothing budget, it seemed, had gone into costumes—a clingy white jersey, a glittery blue and silver creation that still sparkled after so many years, and a strapless black velvet gown that looked as if it should be worn by royalty.

A note from her mother's landlady, one Marie Arnogne, had accompanied Solange's personal belongings back to Carteret. But beyond the woman's name, it offered little information.

Annie raised her eyes to her cousin's. "Is this all?"

He nodded. "Nearly everythin' she had went to pay for her care. She . . . died of acute leukemia, you know."

As a tear rolled down Annie's cheek, Zenon awkwardly handed her his handkerchief. "It's 'most time for my father to return," he said. "Maybe it would be . . . uh, better if I broke the news about your visit after you've gone. Is there anythin' else I can do to help?"

"Can you think of someone in New Orleans who might remember her?" she asked, refusing to be put off just yet by his nervousness. "What about the boarding-house where she lived, and the club where she sang? Do you know if they're still there?"

Zenon shook his head. "I doubt if your mother's landlady is alive," he said. "But the boardin' house is still on Esplanade Street, at the edge of the Quarter. The club is called Paradise Lost these days." He paused, then added with a faint smile that perceptibly softened his somber face, "I had a drink there last time I was in town."

Did her reserved banker cousin share the family's

secret passion for jazz? Annie wondered. Or had he gone to the little club out of nostalgia and an interest in family history? At the moment, there wasn't time to find out. She didn't want to press her luck—or make Zenon Trosclair uncomfortable. "I suppose I'd better be going," she said tentatively, getting to her feet.

Her cousin's relief was immediate. "Let me get you a glass of ice water first," he insisted. "You can drink it while I arrange a ride for you into town."

Half an hour later she was seated beside a portly, sweating farmer headed for New Orleans, her baggage loaded on the back of his pickup along with tomatoes and cucumbers and watermelons destined for the produce market there.

"Chemical plants along the river'll be lettin' out," he muttered. "Got to take the back road."

Annie nodded. There was nothing to see along the string-straight highway anyway but willow swamps and a few cars parked at fishing spots. And besides, Annie's mind wasn't on sightseeing. I don't know what I expected to find at Carteret, she thought. Certainly not a welcome. As cordial as her cousin had been, he had made one thing plain—his father would want nothing to do with Solange, not even in memory.

For the first time it struck her that her quest to uncover her mother's past might be doomed to failure. Just the same, she didn't plan to give up easily, even if her search proved at first to be a difficult and lonely one. Leaning her head back against the seat, Annie closed her eyes.

They arrived in New Orleans about suppertime, crossing the soaring Mississippi River Bridge that spread the metropolis at their feet in a glittering blue haze. Directly ahead were the pinnacles of glass and steel that marked the city's center. Instinctively she glanced to her right, in the direction of the Vieux Carré.

They got off the expressway at the next exit. "Where can I drop you, miss?" the truck farmer asked.

"Bourbon and St. Peter streets, if that's all right." She was staring out the window at the crowds, the traffic, the huge restlessness of the biggest city she had ever seen.

He shrugged. "I guess I can. That place is a madhouse in the evenings, though."

The narrow streets of the French Quarter closed around them, constricted by traffic and lined with shops and restaurants and lacy iron balconies. Several minutes later they halted at a clogged corner, and Annie saw immediately what he had meant. People of all ages and backgrounds were strolling down the middle of Bourbon Street, which was closed off to vehicular traffic. Boys were tap dancing on the pavement to the strains of some classical jazz that drifted out of one of the clubs; a cigar box for contributions was at their feet. A man was shilling rides in a horse-drawn carriage.

Annie got out and hoisted down her two suitcases, just barely remembering to thank the driver as she gazed about her, wide-eyed. The next moment she was jumping back onto the curb to avoid a small foreign convertible that had pulled up to take the vegetable truck's place.

Across the street was the source of the tap dancers' music and her first destination in the city—the former Red Door, now the Paradise Lost. As she crossed to the opposite side, she saw that the musicians inside the club were finishing their set and beginning a break. The crowd that had gathered at the open doorway was dispersing. Careful not to bump into anyone with her bags, Annie edged closer to have a look inside.

My mother sang here, she thought, noting the crowded stage, the clutter of round, marble-topped tables and bentwood chairs, and the massive mahogany bar with its oil painting of a jazz funeral above the forest of bottles and glasses. Barely visible in back of the club was a courtyard with a little fountain.

She wondered how much the place had changed in the intervening years. Then her gaze slid back to the bandstand, where one of the musicians, the drummer, had remained behind to light a cigarette and joke with the bass player. To her surprise, Annie experienced a tingle of recognition though she was certain she'd never seen him before.

He wasn't handsome in the usual sense. His features were too irregular for that. She noted neatly cropped dark hair and mobile, emphatic brows, little lines around his mouth that suggested a mercurial and none-too-innocent smile.

In his mid to late thirties, he was well built but only of medium height, perhaps two or three inches taller than she. He was no fashion plate, either, if his nondescript slacks and rolled-up shirt sleeves were any indication.

Yet for all that, there was something extraordinary about him—a certain indefinable quality that must always place him at the center of things, she decided with sudden insight.

He would be the leader of the quintet and an excellent musician, she guessed, the member of the group most ready with banter and comebacks for the crowd. She sensed that he was a man well liked and admired, at ease in the tough, competitive world of jazz music. She had dreamed of just such a man the night of her father's funeral, she realized.

Annie came to herself with a little start, aware that she was staring. The dark-haired drummer was aware of it too. "Next set in a few minutes, honey," he called casually in her direction, favoring her with the uneven, slightly wicked grin she'd known he possessed. "Come on in and sit down."

Annie flushed, not knowing what to say. Despite her discomfort, she had to admit that the stranger's a- mused, confident air did nothing to lessen his attractive- ness.

That's the kind of man who wouldn't put you in a box, her inner self prompted. Probably the kind your mother knew well. You couldn't pin *him* down if you tried.

"Don' mind Jake," said a voice at her elbow. "Jivin' the tourists comes with the territory."

She turned to find herself face-to-face with the group's elderly piano player. Wreathed in smoke from his own cigarette, he was grinning at her.

Annie couldn't help smiling back. "I'm not a tourist," she replied. "It's just that I . . . these suitcases . . ."

He nodded, his teeth white against the ebony of his face. "You lookin' for a job, then?" he asked.

"Well, yes. Actually I am. I came here first because my mother used to sing in this place."

One of the old man's eyebrows lifted a little. "Any- body I would know?"

Hopefully, Annie gave her mother's name, then added her own.

The piano player, who introduced himself as Oscar Washington, shook his head. "Sorry," he admitted. "Don' remember her. So happens we're lookin' for a singer here. Guess you better do like Jake suggested, if you're interested. He's the one you have to see."

2

Annie glanced quickly at the drummer, who was putting out his cigarette and tossing it aside in a little arc. I'll have to deal with him if I want to perform on the stage where my mother sang, she thought. The idea had a certain appeal—even if their brief exchange across the room had left her with a distinct feeling of vulnerability. She had the strong impression that he was a man who knew what he wanted and usually got it, a trait she found both admirable and a little daunting.

Striving to appear poised, she turned back to Oscar Washington. "Him?" she asked as offhandedly as she could. "I thought he was just one of the musicians."

The old man laughed and shook his head. "Never heard Jake described like that," he admitted. "Oh, he sits in with us now and then. But if you want the truth, he's part owner of this place . . . along with Harry Wilson, who writes for the newspaper."

Annie's eyes widened a little. "He must be some drummer if he can afford his own club," she acknowledged.

Oscar nodded, the smile never leaving his face. "That he is, honey. But he comes from a wealthy family. And he's got another job, too . . . drawin' up fancy buildin' plans."

"You mean he's an architect?"

"That's right. You comin' in? It's 'most time for another show."

She couldn't refuse. There was nothing she wanted more at the moment than to sit at one of the little tables and drink in the atmosphere of this place where her mother had performed so long ago.

You want to hear Jake too, she added. Admit it—he's got your attention.

"All right," she replied, earning Oscar's smiling approval. "I really do want to talk to your friend if there's a job open. Do you think you could arrange it?"

The piano player stretched out his hands for her suitcases. "I'll send him over after the next set," he promised. "Jus' tell the waitress you're a friend of mine, so she won' charge you four-fifty for a glass of soda."

The members of the quintet were drifting back to the bandstand as Annie took a seat. She ordered a gin and tonic, and sipped it as they began to play.

Though Jake was obviously the leader, she could see that he let the front instruments have their say. He might be good—even better than good—yet he gave them exactly the kind of backup they required, just the correct riffs and background rhythm, with a subtlety that barely hinted at what he could do.

I'd like to see what he's like on a solo, she thought,

noting his thorough enjoyment of the music and his keen involvement in the others' playing. I'll bet he's really something. She couldn't help warming to his spontaneous little gestures, the way those small, curving lines beside his mouth came into play.

He was in good company. The other members of the group weren't lacking in talent either, even by the standards of this town where jazz was a native art. The thin black youth on the trumpet had both fire and restraint, while Oscar's large, bony hands slipped over the piano keys as loosely and easily as if he'd been doing it for a hundred years. The middle-aged saxo-phonist, a large, affable man, played with verve and style. And the intense, wild-haired boy on bass fingered his battered instrument with skilled affection.

How I'd love to sing with them, Annie thought, losing herself in their playing. She knew all too well that her slender store of experience—mainly the gig she'd done without her father's knowledge at an off-campus bar—wouldn't count for much here. Yet she had what it took; she believed in that implicitly. If only she could get Jake to audition her, she might have a chance.

From the first number, the quintet segued into a whole string of thirties' and forties' favorites. They're playing the kind of music I love, she thought, feeling her excitement rise. I'm exactly the right person to sing with them. If only I can convince them of that.

There was a brisk round of applause at the end of the medley, and then the group launched into one of Annie's all-time favorites, a slow, romantic tune she had spied among the sheet music in Solange's suitcase. It was a perfect song for a "canary" to show her stuff. They were playing the first run-through all smooth and sentimental, and Annie found herself silently filling in the words. She could imagine herself on the bandstand beside them, weaving vocal variations while she cradled the mike like a baby.

The drummer was watching her, his eyes narrowed slightly under those dark brows. What might have been a look of recognition passed between them as she became aware of his attention. The corners of his mouth curved a little as his gaze continued to hold hers. She had the sudden, improbable notion that he had deliberately chosen the song, with its familiar lyrics, as a continuation of the dialogue between them.

Lost for a moment in the lyrics, she gave herself a mental shake. Of course, it was all a game, probably just part of jiving the tourists, as Oscar had told her. Yet involuntarily her lips parted, and he flashed her that maddeningly confident grin, as if to confirm that she had understood him well enough. As if in mockery, the music took off in a hot jazz application of the theme.

Certain she was flushing again, Annie refused to look away; she applauded harder than anyone when he concluded a brief, hard-driving solo just before the reprise.

At the end of the set, Annie saw Oscar talking to the drummer, nodding in her direction. She consciously ordered another drink she didn't want, knowing that if he came over to her table, she would definitely need something to do with her hands.

A moment later he *was* coming over. Somewhat taller than he had seemed on the bandstand, he was smiling that faintly lopsided smile and lighting another cigarette. Oscar was with him. And the ability she'd always relied on to remain detached where men were concerned seemed suddenly to have deserted her.

"Annie Duprez, Jake St. Arnold," the piano player said without much ceremony.

"Hello," she said.

"My pleasure." His voice was deep and pleasantly rough about the edges. To her consternation, Jake took her hand, then just stood there looking at her with a pleased yet faintly dubious expression. She couldn't think of anything else to say.

Watching him on the bandstand, she had wondered at the color of his eyes and guessed that they might be hazel. Now she realized how far she'd been from the mark. Beneath their straight dark lashes, they were most definitely blue—the color of a lake. And he used them forthrightly, as if he never felt the need to hide what was on his mind.

At close range, he was even more attractive than she'd thought, with a strong physical magnetism that was impossible to ignore. He had that Gallic air about him she knew to be typical of the best French-Creole heritage, one that fitted perfectly with his anglicized surname. And he positively radiated confidence, an amused if somewhat disillusioned view of the world.

"Oscar tells me your mother used to sing here," he prompted, letting go of her hand as if he knew that to hold it any longer would be disconcerting in the extreme.

"Oh," she said. "Yes. Her name was Solange Duprez. I have a clipping here . . ."

Reaching into her purse, she pulled out the yellowing *Times-Picayune* story. Jake St. Arnold scanned it with quick interest. "You're right," he said, handing it back to her, one tanned, well-shaped hand brushing against hers in the process. "This place used to be known as The Red Door, though it's been called perhaps a dozen other things since. Your mother's name seems familiar, though I can't quite place her. Harry might know. That's Harry Wilson, my partner. He's music and drama critic at the *Times*."

She nodded. "Oscar told me. I'd appreciate it very much if you'd mention her name to him."

"I'd be happy to. But you can ask him yourself, if you want. He'll be around here tomorrow afternoon. We're interviewing for a singer."

"I told Annie 'bout that." Oscar had stepped in before she could say a word. "She's a singer too," he explained.

One brow quirking a little, Jake glanced down at her suitcases. "Looking for a job?" he asked. "Seems to me your most pressing need is a place to sleep."

Surely he hadn't intended an undertone of invitation. "Not to worry," she responded. "I'm planning to rent a room."

He didn't lose his amused expression. "Any singing experience?"

"Not much. I've . . . been teaching music in grade school. But I did sing with a jazz group in college. If you'll give me a chance, I promise you won't be disappointed."

Even as she spoke the words, she realized he'd probably heard them a thousand times. But this unconventionally handsome, blue-eyed man didn't let on to that.

"Sure, why not audition?" he told her, shrugging again in what was doubtless a characteristic gesture. "If you're good, we both have everything to gain. Probably I should warn you, though. The job doesn't pay much and it's only three nights a week. We're looking for somebody with a feeling for swing music that's more than skin-deep. We don't want any rock interpretations."

She refrained from telling him that swing was her specialty. Let him find that out tomorrow, she thought. "I understand," she said.

"Three o'clock, then. Wear something appropriate."

They chatted a little longer, Annie still somewhat tongue-tied, until it was time for Jake and Oscar to step back up to the bandstand again. She sat there a few moments more, just watching him and trying not to show her fascination, as she sipped the remainder of her drink.

Much as she wanted to stay, it was getting late and she really did need to find a room, at least for the night. Praying he wouldn't notice, she stood and picked up her suitcases, trying to move unobtrusively to the door.

But he did notice, and just as she'd feared, he couldn't resist the opportunity. "Don't forget, Annie Duprez," he called after her, not missing a beat. "We've got a rendezvous."

Outside on the crowded pavement, Annie instinctively headed for the boardinghouse where her mother had stayed. It was a long walk to Esplanade Street, through a somewhat rundown residential section of the Quarter. Her bags had become heavy indeed by the time she located the Oakleaf Residence and struggled up its steeply pitched steps to ring the bell.

A plump, gray-haired woman answered.

"Mrs. Arnogne?" Annie asked hopefully.

The woman shook her head. "Sorry, dear," she said with faint traces of an English accent. "Nobody by that name at this address. I'm Sabrina Johnson. I'm the manager here. Would you like to come inside and look at a phone directory? Perhaps the person you're looking for lives somewhere in the neighborhood."

Annie tried not to show her disappointment. There would be time enough later to ask questions about the former landlady. "Actually," she said, "I'm looking for a room. Someone told me a Mrs. Arnogne was the one to see. But it doesn't make any difference. I still need a place to stay."

Sabrina Johnson studied her for a moment. Evidently she passed inspection, for the woman's round face softened with the beginnings of a smile. "We do have a vacancy," she said, wiping her hands on her apron. "A sleeping room with refrigerator, hot plate and private bath. Seventy-five dollars. Payable by the week."

"All right." Suddenly overwhelmed by the events of the day, Annie was in no frame of mind to bargain.

Her new landlady clucked sympathetically. "I imagine you'll want to see it first, before you decide, dearie," she said, leading the way up the stairs.

The room, on the third floor of the old house, was about what Annie had expected. Furnished with a collection of tired-looking and mismatched pieces, it featured a white iron bedstead with a lumpy mattress, and a window that opened out over the rooftops. Off beyond the Bourbon Street enclave and the residential section of the old Quarter, the skyscrapers of downtown New Orleans glittered under luminous clouds.

"I'll take it," Annie said, setting her suitcases down on the pine board floor and digging into her purse.

After Sabrina Johnson had gone, Annie opened the window and leaned out over the sill, unable to believe she was really there, in the city where her mother had come to try her wings. Perhaps this is the very room where she slept, Annie thought.

Had she also found someone like Jake St. Arnold waiting for her here? Was there a dark-haired man with laughing, dangerous eyes who had intruded into her dreams?

With a little sigh, she turned away from the window, stripped off her skirt and blouse and stretched out on the bed. Moments later, she was fast asleep.

Morning came, and with it determination to land the job at Paradise Lost. One way to make sure that happens is to look the part, she thought, deciding to take her courage in hand and lighten her shoulder-length hair. She dug out the kit she'd packed in her suitcase and headed for the bathroom.

The messy process—one she'd performed countless times for her college roommates but never dared to use on herself—was somehow satisfying to her soul. Lighter tresses might give her more stage presence. And she hoped it would be good for her ego to deal with Jake St. Arnold as a blonde.

Forty-five minutes later, she stood before the bathroom's cracked and clouded mirror, surveying her handiwork. Her hair, which she usually wore in a conservative upsweep, was a sun-kissed halo about her shoulders. To accompany the change, she had applied her makeup with a more lavish hand than had been customary for her as a teacher in the local parish schools.

The effect was startling. I look more like Solange than ever, Annie thought, not needing the faded black-and-white photograph now to make a comparison. Much more slowly she came to another realization. Why, I'm almost beautiful, she decided in growing astonishment, meeting her own gray eyes.

Just one problem remained—how to dress for her interview with Jake and his partner. "Wear something appropriate," he'd told her. But she wasn't sure she had brought anything appropriate for the stage of a jazz club. For the past several years her wardrobe had run to sensible separates like those worn by most of the other teachers she'd known. And her few party clothes were too demure and unsophisticated, the sort of things that would make her look like an ingenue all over again.

I have no idea where to shop here in this city, she admitted to herself with a shake of her head. Then she had a sudden inspiration.

It was a little crazy even to consider wearing a twenty-year-old outfit that had spent most of its life in the Trosclair attic. Yet she wasn't about to dismiss the idea without due consideration.

With the faintly shaky feeling that going through her mother's things seemed to give her, she sorted out the valise's contents. Solange hadn't possessed much that was suitable for daytime wear. But there was one possibility—a strapless fitted sheath in crisp, silvery gray rayon with a white pique cuff topping the bodice. Its matching pique-trimmed jacket had been narrowly cut for a tiny waist.

Thanks to the few pounds she'd lost during the stressful week of her father's funeral, the dress slid without effort over her slender hips and thighs, and zipped easily past her trim waistline.

Old as it was, it seemed made for her—even the color, which emphasized her eyes and matched the gray sling-back pumps she'd brought from home, spiky ones that did wonders for her legs. I'll have to put my hair back up though, she decided. It's much too young looking like this, hanging about my ears.

That afternoon, she was neatly turned out if a little nervous as she arrived at Paradise Lost, her hair caught up in a forties' do that oddly enough complemented her sixties' outfit. Today the club was officially closed, though one wood-framed glass door stood ajar.

Pushing it open, she walked in. Jake was nowhere in sight. There was a cleaning woman mopping up, and a sandy-haired man in jeans and a tee shirt at one of the tables was going over some books.

"Hello," she said a bit tentatively. "I'm Annie Duprez . . ."

The sandy-haired man looked up and smiled. "You must be the singer," he said, getting up at once and holding out his hand. "I'm Harry Wilson. Jake is upstairs, and Oscar's out back having a cigarette. Excuse me while I get them together."

His grip was friendly and firm. Annie liked him immediately, all the more perhaps because no uncomfortable man-woman thing sparked between them.

A moment later Harry was back, followed by a beaming Oscar Washington. "Jake's on the phone," Harry said. "He'll be right with us."

Dimming the house lights, he flipped on several of the overhead spots, then took a chair at one of the tables while Oscar sat down at the piano. "Ready whenever you are," he told her.

Cautiously Annie stepped up onstage, tapped the mike. It was live. "What'll it be?" Oscar asked in a paternal, reassuring tone.

She named a slow, sensuous, almost torchy song, guessing that he played by ear and didn't require a score.

"'Bout here?" He offered her a few bars that ended on a blue note, unerringly perfect for her range.

Making a circle with thumb and forefinger, Annie tried to quell the butterflies in her stomach as the pianist rippled through the song's introduction. As always, her nervousness vanished as soon as she lost herself in the music.

She spontaneously inserted some jazz phrasing. Instantly Oscar was with her, giving her the backup she required. Hinting at a scat vocal on the reprise, she could feel it working better than she had any right to hope. Through the medium of the song, her own aspirations and her loneliness in the new life she'd chosen seemed lifted to incredible heights.

Out of the corner of her eye she saw Jake come in. Willing herself not to be thrown off by his presence, she went even deeper into the music. But she was only half-aware of how good it was, how satin-smooth her brassy notes, or how lush the rough ones were, like velvet stroked against the grain.

Finished, she just dropped her hands at her sides. Silence filled the room. Didn't they like it? she wondered. Then Harry broke the tension with applause. Her accompanist joined in.

Only Jake seemed to be withholding judgment. Stepping nearer, he stood a few feet from the stage. He was wearing tennis shorts in white cotton that revealed his powerful legs; a tan cotton safari shirt was open at the collar. And there were man-woman sparks this time just as there had been the night before—enough to light up the room.

"Very nice, angel," he drawled, his voice soft and yet faintly abrasive in the way she remembered. "You gave that song every ounce of talent and feeling it deserves. But your performance was somehow at odds with the music."

"At odds?" The unexpected criticism threw her off-balance. "What . . . what do you mean?"

"Jake . . ." Harry was on his feet, ready, she guessed, to defend her. But she could handle this herself.

"I don't understand," she added more steadily. "Please explain."

He shrugged. "I don't know. The song was wonderful. But your total performance was somehow . . . *prim,* as if you were letting go only in the music. I'm sorry, but that's the impression I got. Perhaps it's that jacket . . . and your hair . . ."

Before Annie could protest, he was on the stage beside her. Blunt, capable fingers were removing her jacket, releasing the weight of her hair from its hairpins. The back of his hand, accidentally brushing against her cheek, caused a little shiver to run along her spine.

"That's more like it," he said, lowering his voice as he arranged her hair so that it slanted across her forehead in a style she recognized as a 'Veronica Lake.'

His mouth was so close to hers that she imagined she could feel the faint warmth of his breath. How would it feel, she asked herself, her concern sliding into confusion, if he pressed that curving, sensual mouth down on mine?

Then he drew back a little, still giving her that crooked smile. "Even the look on your face is right now," he said with satisfaction. "Let's give it another try."

3

Oscar was already running through the opening bars as Jake stepped down to take a seat squarely in front of the mike.

"Go ahead," he encouraged. "Sing it right to me."

Annie was embarrassed at the suggestion her performance had been too ladylike, but she had to admit that in a sense he was right. From the moment she had walked into Paradise Lost that afternoon, she had been holding herself back, as if she were afraid of something.

Maybe it's coming face-to-face with my dream and wondering if I'll be good enough, she thought. Or maybe it's Jake. I'd be wise to take care. A man like him could upset all my plans.

Still, if a *sexy* performance was what he wanted, she would give it to him. That was the way he made her feel, anyway. She was brimming with the emotions he'd evoked simply by touching her cheek and standing too near. She was also a little annoyed with herself for being so susceptible.

I'll show him who's prim, she vowed, unwilling to have him think of her as inexperienced or a prude. She realized with a start that Oscar had begun the introduction for the second time.

"Annie?" Jake was asking.

"All right," she said.

I'm going to let out what he makes me feel, she decided, catching up the song's first husky notes. And I'll get this job if it's the last thing I do.

Something broke free in her at the resolve. Reveling in a sensuality she hadn't fully known she possessed, she belted out the lament of a woman so wild about her man she would take him on any terms. She had a good body—Jake's admiring glances confirmed that. Now she used it to the fullest, swishing her loose hair about her shoulders, turning on the full candlepower of her large gray eyes. Even her hips in the arrow-straight skirt arched subtly forward, as if her movements were rehearsing the act of love.

Wantonly she imagined herself in Jake's arms, her fingers tangling in his thick dark hair as he pulled her up against him to cover her mouth with his.

But the song was a blues number, after all. Like it or not, she had to picture him setting her aside as the music ended, had to portray for her audience the ache of rejection. Again when she finished, no one spoke. Well, it was good, Annie thought, searching their faces. I know that.

Finally Jake broke the silence. His voice was solemn, almost respectful, though his beautiful eyes held anything but reverence. He didn't praise her. "Do an encore," he requested. "Surprise me."

Later she couldn't have said why she chose a folk tune her father had sometimes sung or played on the harmonica. Perhaps she had simply taken Jake at his word and attempted to surprise him, knowing he wouldn't expect her to follow the deep sensuality of the blues number with a song so candid and simple it could be sung by a child.

"You may not have heard this before," she warned, breaking eye contact with him as she turned back toward the piano player. "Just follow as best you can."

Oscar's gleaming dark face showed polite disbelief that there could be a song he didn't know. Yet though he probably hadn't heard this one before, Annie wasn't terribly surprised when he picked up enough of the melody to accompany her. Softly the plaintive Cajun lyric floated out into the air. She gave them innocence this time, as a foil for what had gone before.

She sang only a few of the song's many verses, paused for just the space of a heartbeat after the last note faded, then broke into a no-holds-barred version of a jazz favorite.

"That's it!" Oscar exclaimed as he let loose on the piano.

Confidence filled her in a joyous surge. At that moment, she felt thoroughly in control of the voice that was her instrument, able to hit the brassiest high notes without faltering, plumb with ease the depths of her register. Just as Jake had been the day before, she was totally present in her music, alive beyond the usual sense in doing what she did best.

Harry shook his head as she finished. "That was

merely sensational," he said, glancing over at his partner. "As far as I'm concerned, she's hired."

Oscar grinned broadly as he hushed a boy about eight or nine years old who had wandered in to stand beside him. Annie glanced at Jake, who was regarding her with a speculative expression.

"I agree," he said finally, getting to his feet. "Shall we have a drink to celebrate? Or just go back to the office and talk terms? I assume you want the job, Annie."

Harry had come up to give her hand a reassuring squeeze. "I hope to hell she does," he laughed. "We're lucky she turned up on our doorstep."

Jake grinned. "That remark is going to cost us, you know. As I said, angel . . . the job's yours if you want it: on a trial basis now, permanently if things work out to our mutual satisfaction. What do you say?"

It was the second time he'd called her *angel*. Despite the fact that it was probably a habitual nickname with him, she couldn't help the little fluttery feeling it gave her—any more than she could help wondering if there was a double meaning to his words about mutual satisfaction.

Meanwhile, he was waiting for an answer. Though he hadn't mentioned anything specific about salary, she didn't really need to think things over. She wanted this job on any terms.

"Yes," she responded, for the first time giving him her shy smile. "I want to work for you."

Something wary flickered in his eyes, but "Good," was all he said as he tucked her jacket over her arm. "Oscar, come join us. Drinks are on the house."

Obviously pleased at the turn of events, the piano player shook his head. "Wish I could," he said. "But I promised my grandson Dabney, here, I'd teach him to shoot pool this afternoon. That's some voice you got, Annie. I'm proud to be workin' with you, girl."

"Same here." Warmly she shook the large, bony hand he offered. "I just hope I can measure up to your playing."

Oscar's smile broadened. "Oh, you will. Jake'll see to that." Then he left, his arm draped across the youngster's shoulder.

"Oscar's raising him," Jake explained. "And doing a damn fine job of it."

Before he could go on, the phone rang at the far end of the bar and Harry went to answer it. Annie glanced after Oscar and his grandson. "I'm sure you're right," she replied. "I already think the world of Oscar, you know."

Perched on a high old-fashioned stool in front of the club's mahogany bar, she watched as Jake put her gin and tonic together and poured an expensive brand of Scotch for himself and his partner.

"What have you done to your hair?" he asked abruptly as he handed over her drink. "And that dress . . . it's like something out of an old movie."

So much for glamour, she thought. "The dress was my mother's," she confessed. "Probably I shouldn't have worn it. But I didn't really have anything else. And I . . . guess I thought my hair was too drab to make an impression."

Unexpectedly Jake tilted her chin with one hand. "Don't apologize," he said. "I *like* your dress. And your hair is like sunlight today. But even when you came in all tired and dusty with your suitcases yesterday, you made a better impression than you knew."

She was flushing again when Harry returned to take a seat beside her. He didn't seem to notice, or to get the idea he'd interrupted anything. "I'd like to propose a toast," he said, raising his glass. "To Miss Annie Duprez. May our association with her be long and prosperous."

"Hear, hear." With a half-serious salute in her direction, Jake raised his glass. Though he had stepped back a little at Harry's approach, Annie could still feel his gaze on her like a touch.

There isn't any doubt about the risk he represents, she thought. I'd be in over my depth with him.

"Where did you learn to sing like that?" Harry was asking in his amiable way.

She smiled. "I hope you mean that as a compliment, since you've just hired me. I guess I picked up the songs from old records, mostly, when I was in college. I had a boyfriend who was a disc jockey on a late-night jazz show. He introduced me to swing, but it wasn't really like an introduction at all . . . more like meeting something that had always been a part of me."

"Well, you gave one hell of a performance."

"Thank you."

Jake was watching her intently. "I know what you mean," he said, putting down his glass on the counter and resting his hand beside it. "About finding your style that way. But you sang at least one number that didn't come from any jazz program."

She knew which one he meant. "I got the French song from my father," she said.

"It's Cajun, isn't it?"

Annie nodded. "I guess he sang it because it was like a commentary on his life." And then she wondered why she'd confided so readily in this stranger.

45

Jake was giving her a quizzical look. "Your mother left him?" he asked.

So he understood the Cajun dialect. "That's right. For her career . . . when I was small. I don't actually remember her."

He turned to Harry. "I meant to tell you," he said. "Annie is trying to find out what she can about her mother, Solange Duprez. She used to sing here at the club in the early sixties."

"Well, I'll be damned." Harry drew his sandy brows together. "Afraid I can't place the name, though it sounds familiar. What kind of stuff did she sing?"

For the most part, Annie managed to keep her voice free of emotion as she related what little she knew. "Like her, I've always wanted to sing," she concluded. "With my father gone, there wasn't any reason not to give it a try. But that's only part of why I came to New Orleans. I wanted to find someone who knew Solange, find out what she was really like. Make my peace with her, I suppose you could say."

Jake nodded gravely, for once abandoning his a-mused, ironic air. His partner was leaning forward with interest. "That's quite a story," Harry said. "One worth doing for the paper once you get launched in our city. Since I'll be one of your employers, I couldn't write it myself. Conflict of interest, you know. But we might assign it to someone."

"Without any information on Solange, half the story would be missing," Annie said, trying not to let him raise her hopes too much.

"I don't see why," Jake put in thoughtfully. "A story about the search itself might cause someone to come forward."

"You could be right." Harry drained his glass. "But we couldn't do that; it would set a precedent. You have no idea how many other people there are in this city who are looking for lost relatives."

"Then there isn't much use, is there?" Annie looked from Harry to Jake and back again. "Because I can't tell you very much."

"Maybe you won't have to. There may be something in the morgue—the newspaper library, to you. It has clippings from back issues, filed by name, that go much farther back than your mother's time. I can give it a try."

"I'd really appreciate that."

Silent throughout the little exchange, Jake now seemed to give himself a little shake. "Annie," he said. "I almost forgot to tell you. Last night I remembered where I'd seen your mother's name before—on a record in a carton of oldies I picked up at a flea market last fall. It's a forty-five, and not in very good condition. But you can still hear the voice quite plainly. In fact, it's a lot like yours . . ."

He hesitated at the lost, vulnerable look in her large gray eyes, then added softly, "I'll play it for you later, if you like."

"Oh, yes. I would, very much."

A small silence rested between them. "Paradise Lost is closed tonight," Jake said finally. "Why don't we walk over to the office and discuss a contract? Then we can go up to my place and listen to Annie's mother sing."

Harry made a regretful face. "I'd really enjoy that," he said. "But I'm afraid you'll have to negotiate for both of us. That phone call was from my editor. I have to drive out to Baton Rouge tonight on a story. Annie

. . . watch yourself with this man. And call me at the paper tomorrow afternoon. I may have something on Solange by then.''

"I will. And thanks.''

"I'm glad things worked out.''

"So am I.''

Harry closed up the books he'd been going over at her arrival and carried them back across the courtyard to the office he shared with Jake. Moments later, he was backing his sports car out of its private parking space. She and Jake remained standing outside beside the splashing fountain with its bronze sculpture of two children huddled under an oversized umbrella.

Annie glanced around the flagstone-paved courtyard with its ragged, tender banana plants and crumbling pots of geraniums. "What a charming spot,'' she remarked, feeling a bit self-conscious at being alone with him.

"I like it,'' Jake said quietly.

She trailed her hand in the water of the fountain, not meeting his eyes. "I can't help wondering about this bronze, though,'' she added. "The subject seems more appropriate for a nursery school than a nightclub.''

His face took on a shuttered look. "Maybe so,'' he said. "But I put it there myself. The fact is, I like children . . . even had one of my own.''

She'd already noticed that he didn't wear a wedding ring. And though that wasn't necessarily significant, from the faraway sound in his voice, she guessed he wasn't married now. Divorced, then, she concluded, wondering why she was happy at the notion. Yet it made her a little sad, too, thinking he must rarely see the child he'd spoken about.

When she didn't say anything, he leaned back against the sun-warmed archway that led to his office, regarding her with narrowed eyes in the brilliant, late-afternoon light.

"We might as well negotiate out here," he said, lighting a cigarette and naming a figure that was too generous for three nights a week, though it still wouldn't be enough to support her on a long-term basis.

He wasn't flirting with her at the moment. Even so, she felt drawn to him even more strongly now that they were alone. She couldn't help noticing the shape of his mouth or the way his open-necked shirt revealed a slim dark triangle of chest hair. Thanks to his relaxed posture, his light, beautiful eyes were almost on a level with hers; they seemed to seek out her innermost thoughts.

Pay attention, Annie reminded herself. This is business, after all. "I consider that a fair offer," she said, striving for equanimity.

The corners of his mouth lifted a little. "You're much too easily persuaded. But I won't protest. You're aware that we'll want a standard contract, with a penalty for nonperformance, the usual permission to use your name in advertisements, along with a publicity photograph . . ."

Strands of hair were blowing about her face, and Annie tucked them absently behind one ear. "I'm afraid I don't have any," she said.

"You'll need to get some taken, then." Pulling out his wallet, he extracted several business cards and gave one to her. "Here's the phone number of a friend of mine who's a photographer. Call and make an appointment for tomorrow or the next day." He paused, his expression thoughtful, then handed her another card. "This is my other office number. I'm an architect during regular working hours. Let me know what arrangements you make."

His friend's card, printed on pale blue stock, stated the owner's name and profession with stark simplicity: *Y.L. Carr, Photography*. Annie gazed somewhat longer at Jake's, with its sienna-brown logo on a cream-colored ground. It proclaimed his rather formidable full name and credentials: *Ashley Jacobsen St. Arnold, A.I.A.*

"Any suggestions about what I should wear for the photograph?" she asked.

He grinned. "Sure. Your sexiest evening dress. With your hair slanting across your forehead in that suggestive way."

She wasn't quite sure how to reply to that. "When do I start?" she asked, retreating into the safety of business arrangements.

"I didn't tell you that, did I? How about Saturday night? We should be able to get an ad in the paper by then."

A tiny butterfly of apprehension took flight. "I really should practice . . ."

"You can do that mornings with Oscar, if you'd like. He lives next to my office in the first-floor apartment facing onto St. Peter Street. But any practice with the full group would have to take place after hours . . . at about three a.m. on Thursday or Saturday mornings."

Her eyes must have widened at the outlandish schedule. "Well, you said you wanted a singing career," he reminded her, flashing that lopsided smile. "Better cultivate some night-owl proclivities if you plan to survive. Listen, our business is settled. Why don't we go upstairs to my place so I can put on that record for you?"

With only the slightest hesitation, Annie agreed, preceding him up a narrow flight of wrought-iron steps to his second-floor apartment. As she stepped inside, she was not prepared for the beauty before her, a very personal beauty that in some way seemed to express the man.

Painted a neutral off-white, the walls rose to a high ceiling that gave the room a spacious, airy feeling. White ceramic tiles cooled the floor, which was warmed by the counterpoint of a Tabriz rug in soft beiges and siennas and blues. Defining the clean-swept hearth, with its heavy brass and irons, was the delicate, pared-down pattern of a Calder mobile—an original, she was certain. A ram's head Directoire chair and two plush sofas were upholstered in a velvety sand color. Art and flowers were everywhere: framed sketches and water-color portraits of jazz greats, a bewildering variety of orchids in lush creams and cerises, pinks and pale golds, that he must have grown himself. At one end of the room a spiral mahogany and iron stair led upward toward what Annie guessed was the bedroom. An arching window, half shuttered, admitted glimpses of the greenery below.

"It's wonderful!" she blurted, adding to herself that if the room were any further removed in style and ambiance from the cottage on Bayou Black, it would have to be on another planet.

One dark eyebrow lifted. "Thanks," he responded in a faintly self-deprecating tone. "It's home. Please . . . make yourself comfortable. I noticed that you didn't finish your drink downstairs. Can I get you something else? I have iced tea already made in the refrigerator."

"Tea would be lovely." She sank into the luxurious depths of one of the sofas. "No sugar. And plenty of lemon, if that's all right."

"Just tell me your heart's desire." Disappearing briefly behind a pair of louvered swinging doors, he returned a moment later with the tea in tall crystal glasses.

"Drink up," he advised, placing his own glass on the low table in front of her. "I'll put on the record."

Jake's stereo was concealed in a cabinet that was similar in style to the ram's head chair. In its eclectic surroundings, it took on a curiously art deco look. He slipped Solange's record out of its protective jacket. "Delta label," he said. "Backup by a group called the Bourbon Street Five. I hope you're not disappointed in the quality."

He put the disc on the turntable, then came over to sit beside her. At first, the cartridge picked up nothing but static and the slow *tic-tic-tic* of what was probably a scratch across the grooves. Then the opening bars of a bittersweet Lena Horne favorite floated out into the room. A voice remarkably like Annie's own took up the melody.

A shiver went through her that had nothing to do with cold. She sat transfixed, gripping her glass with such force that Jake lifted it gently out of her hands and set it aside.

It seemed almost a miracle. She was listening to Solange. Across the more than twenty-three years that had gone by since Annie had nestled in her lap as a baby, the twenty years or so that had passed since her death, her mother's voice reached into this room.

How talented she was, Annie acknowleged, heedless of the tears that were streaming down her cheeks. And how doomed. The unhappiness she was singing about was real.

Still she found she couldn't bring herself to forgive the woman who was singing so eloquently of despair. This was the angel who had broken her father's heart.

Annie listened, fascinated, as Solange abandoned the song's slow, bluesy rhythm for a magnificent scat vocal. Abruptly, the tempo slowed again, and the voice from the past broke a little with emotion as the tune slid into a reprise. It isn't Ned she was singing about, Annie reminded herself, unaware that a little moan had escaped her. She'd had other men. . . .

Silence filled the room as Jake removed the record. With her face buried against one of the sofa cushions, Annie didn't see his look of pain as he returned and took her hands in his.

"Baby . . . ," was all he said.

Drawing her to her feet, he enfolded her. She didn't protest. Safe in the shelter of his arms, she wept without reservation.

She was feeling more than impersonal curiosity about her mother now, all right, more than a desire to make her peace. Solange's voice, so angelic and yet so jaded, had stirred up all the old rejection, every tattered remnant of anger that there had been no wife to ease her father's loneliness; for her, no mother's love.

"Sweetheart, don't." Jake's arms tightened around her. The expressive hands she'd so admired were stroking her hair as tenderly as if she were a child.

Annie hid her face against his shoulder, willing the tears to end. "Please . . . forgive me," she managed. "I'm sorry for being such a fool."

"Don't apologize. Tell me what I can do."

She suppressed a little hiccup. "Just hold me."

It was as if something had changed between them at her words. Without realizing how it had happened, she had slipped her arms around him too. They stood there in the middle of the quiet, beautiful room, his dark head bent to her bright one, those comforting hands straying from her hair to the smooth skin of her back and shoulders.

Warm and practiced, his touch telegraphed an unmistakable message: compassion had given way to desire. She wasn't certain yet that she *wanted* him to want her. Still, the thought that he did ignited little bonfires of longing she didn't want to quell.

"Oh, Jake," she whispered, overcome by feelings too powerful to ignore. Not pausing to consider the consequences, she caressed his back through the soft fabric of his shirt, tangled her fingers in the thick, dark hair at his nape the way she had done earlier in her imagination.

With a sigh of what might have been capitulation, he drew her more closely against him. She could feel the hard outline of his male body, the strong muscles of his thighs pressing against her own. Jake's scent—tangy aftershave blending just perceptibly with the very personal aroma of sun-warmed skin—filled her nostrils.

As if they had always been lovers, he was placing blunt little kisses on her forehead, her cheek. "Annie, Annie," he whispered, his voice rough with emotion. "Don't you know how very good you are to hold?"

Later she would tell herself that had been the watershed—the moment at which she could still have stepped back, made amends for imposing on his hospitality, and disappeared briefly into the bathroom on the pretext of fixing her face.

But doubtless her freedom to resist was by that time

just an illusion. There was an inherent power in Jake St. Arnold that mastered all her defenses, even while it promised refuge.

With him, she wasn't capable of rational thought. Instead, she could only feel—in great waves of longing that swept her further and further out of control. I want him to make love to me, she realized in astonishment. To read my secrets with his body. Rock me in his arms until I forget everything but him.

4

Jake's warm, insistent mouth had come down on hers to nuzzle it with little kisses and gently tease her lips apart. Now, as if he sensed her fantasies of surrender, he deepened his kiss until it seemed as if he would touch the very center of her being. On her breasts, his hands kneaded and caressed, teasing her nipples erect beneath the slubbed, silver-gray fabric of her dress. Any moment, Annie thought breathlessly, and he'll be unzipping it, easing it to the floor.

The possibility pierced her with even sharper arrows of desire. Never before had any man made her want him in this feverish way. It might be against all propriety and reason, but though she'd known him less than a day, and had a history of reserve when it came to men, she was ready to let him undress her, carry her off to a place of cool sheets and glorious communion. . . .

"No," Jake said.

To her amazement and shame, he drew back and gently but firmly disengaged her arms from around his neck. The scenario she had imagined near the end of the blues number was actually taking place.

"I . . . don't understand," she whispered in mortification.

"How could I expect you to?"

With a small gesture of impatience with himself, he turned away, his face wearing its shuttered look again. He busied himself lighting a cigarette.

The action gave her a moment to regain her composure. Embarrassed and once again close to tears, Annie held her ground. With trembling fingers she rearranged her hair, smoothed down her dress. "I think you owe me an explanation," she said, her voice a trifle unsteady despite her best efforts. "It's no secret that you enjoyed . . . what we were doing . . . as much as I."

He shot her a swift look that contained no small amount of surprise. "You're right," he admitted, blowing out a cloud of smoke. "I was. But you're . . . well, not the sort of girl I'd care to inveigle into an affair."

It was her turn to look astonished. "Is that so?" she demanded. "What kind of girl . . . no, woman . . . do you think I am?"

"The nice, decent kind . . . as dangerous as they come. Not to mention passionate and desirable. If you want the truth, I'm sorry I can't take advantage of the latter qualities."

"How very decent you are!"

Jake shook his head. She could see that her sarcastic play on words hadn't been lost on him. "Not particularly," he said. "But I do have my reasons. And I don't expect you to understand them. Please . . . accept my apology. It was my fault we got carried away."

"Really? You strike me as being more perceptive than that." She gathered up her things.

"Annie," he interposed, stopping her at the door. "If you're going to work for me . . . we'll both have to get past what happened here today."

She shrugged off his hand. "Is that still what you want? For me to work for you?"

"Do you have to ask? You're a damn fine singer, whether you know it or not. You'd be an asset to Paradise Lost."

Annie gave him a look. *This has to be one of life's little ironies,* she retorted in scathing silence. *You finally give me the vote of confidence I want as a singer . . . after destroying my equilibrium as a woman.*

As usual, he was standing too near, and she resented that liberty more than she could say. "Well?" he asked in that sensual, rough voice that could make her knees go weak if she'd let it. "You haven't signed on the dotted line yet. Are you going to keep your part of our bargain?"

It's going to be hell working for him after this, she thought, *now that I can guess what it must be like to be his lover.* "All right," she conceded, knowing it was still what she wanted to do. "I'll keep it. But I'll also make you a little promise. Nothing like this is going to happen between us again . . . even if you change your mind."

A shadow of regret veiled his beautiful eyes, but it was there so briefly she couldn't be certain she'd seen it at all. "Fair's fair," he agreed. "Even if I might want to be less than a gentleman and keep my options open. Don't forget to call me after you make your photography appointment. I want to be on hand to orchestrate things."

Annie nodded, trying not to think too much about

what his presence would entail. She already had a fair idea of what he was planning, after the way he'd removed her jacket and unfastened her hair. "Well," she said with a defiant tilt of her chin, "goodbye, then."

"Goodbye," he said.

Jake's door closed behind her. She walked down the narrow, iron-railed steps they had mounted together, her emotions in a precarious state. He had wanted her, that much was certain. And he was determined not to have her, for reasons he'd said were his own.

Meanwhile, though she hadn't made any secret of her own desire, embarrassment was giving way to speculation. He'd told her she was much too nice, too decent—not the sort of woman he would choose for an affair.

To her disgust, she found herself making excuses for him. I'll bet his ex-wife answers to that description, she thought: a prim and proper prude who doesn't know how to keep a man content. Or somebody who thought she was too good for him. He must be so burned that he doesn't want to get involved again—except with the kind of woman he knows from the start he couldn't love.

If any of her guesswork was accurate, he'd paid her an unwitting compliment, one she wasn't so sure she deserved. My performance in Jake's apartment this afternoon just proves I'm not the nice, decent type at all, she thought.

For perhaps the hundredth time since she'd opened Ned Duprez's secret drawer, Annie wondered if she herself was the way she pictured Solange—sensual, a risk taker and a loner, a woman who would leave her man behind in single-minded pursuit of a goal. A seeming angel, she added, the way men at the old Red

Door had visualized her mother. Are we two of a kind, she thought, two women with nothing but ambition for a soul?

Yet there was a flaw in that kind of reasoning that caught at her consciousness the way a cat's claw catches at a sweater, pulling up a loose thread that must be examined and rewoven into the fabric. Hadn't she felt as if all her plans were dissolving as she stood in his embrace? Hadn't Jake's pull been overwhelming, so much so that she could have gone on making love to him forever if he hadn't turned away?

Right now, she didn't need to delve into such questions. Jake *had* turned away, and saved her from herself. At the moment, she had other important business to handle—songs to practice, the inquiries about her mother that she wanted to put to her landlady. There was also the necessity of getting another part-time job.

The fact that her mouth still felt imprinted with Jake's was something she'd just have to ignore.

Annie's talk the next morning with Sabrina Johnson got her nowhere. Though the British-born landlady was only too eager to help when she learned Annie's story, she had little information to offer.

"A new owner bought this place about ten years ago, just before I took over the management," she said, her watery eyes sympathetic behind rimless glasses. "Since then, we've had a complete turnover of tenants. Nobody who's here now would remember Mrs. Arnogne, let alone your mum. I'm sorry."

When asked if Annie could practice on the parlor piano, she proved more helpful. "Sure, dearie, practice all you like . . . provided it's after ten o'clock in the morning and not too late at night. It must be so exciting, having a singing career. I once dreamed about the notion a bit myself."

After speaking to Mrs. Johnson, Annie used the pay phone in the hall to call the photographer's office. A woman's voice answered, at once sultry and business-like.

Stating her name and need for an appointment, Annie added that Jake St. Arnold had asked her to call. Immediately the woman's tone changed. "Ah," she said with thinly disguised interest. "You must be the singer he told me about."

So Jake had already discussed her with this person, who was probably the photographer's secretary. She couldn't help but wonder if they were close.

"That's right," she acknowledged. "I need the appointment as soon as possible."

There was a little pause, the sound of several large pages riffling. "We can accommodate you on Wednesday at ten," the woman said finally. "You have the address. If you like, I'll call Jake and let him know the time."

It was impossible for Annie to keep a certain edge out of her voice. "I'd certainly appreciate that," she replied.

Feeling even more out of sorts than she had the day before, she returned to her room and dressed in one of her more sedate outfits—a white blouse, a beige linen skirt and sensible walking shoes. Yet a little of the new Annie Duprez, jazz singer, was apparent. Her hair was fluffed about her shoulders instead of being drawn up into a conservative style. And there was a certain look in her eyes. . . .

She chose to ignore the changes. You do look nice and quite decent today, she mocked, appraising herself in the mirror. And then she was vowing not to repeat those hateful words to herself again. It was no use thinking about what had happened in Jake's apartment, or yearning after what might have been.

Concentrate on what you came here to do, she encouraged herself. Today, that means getting a second job so you can afford to indulge your fantasies.

Bourbon Street looked different in the morning light. The barriers that kept out vehicular traffic in the evenings were down, and delivery trucks had moved in to disgorge foodstuffs, liquor and goods for all the little shops. Water puddled on the pavements, attesting to the hosing down they had received after the previous night's revelers had gone.

Uncertain where she was headed or exactly what kind of job she was looking for, Annie sauntered along with the morning crowd of camera-laden tourist couples and families. Like them, she stared wide-eyed at the conglomeration of night spots, the numerous restaurants and competing jazz clubs, the shops selling tee shirts, postcards and souvenirs.

She walked as far as Canal Street, then began retracing her steps. Suddenly she spotted a sign in the window of the Jericho Oyster Bar. HELP WANTED, WAITRESS, it read. PART TIME. Stepping close to the glass, she peered inside, decided she rather liked the old-fashioned floor of tiny white octagonal tiles, the dark wood walls, even the menu, which seemed to consist mainly of po' boys, draft beer, and plates of crawfish or oysters.

Why not? she thought. It's an honorable profession. And landing a job now could save a lot of time pounding the pavement. Diffidently, she walked inside, stepped up to the combination lunch counter and bar. A huge man in chefs' whites, wearing the traditional tall, poufed cap, leaned his elbows on the countertop and waited for her to speak.

Giving him her best smile, Annie stated her name and explained that she had come in answer to the sign. "I've never done waitressing before, and I'm on sabbatical for six months from teaching school," she admitted. "I landed a part-time singing job down the street at Paradise Lost. Now I need something else that will fit around my hours."

The fat man stroked his bristly mustache. "All I ever get in here is singers," he complained, with a glance at his only waitress of the moment, a slim, brown-haired girl who was smiling in Annie's direction.

Politely, Annie waited. After several moments, the man grudgingly introduced himself as Bubba Wright and began to explain what the job entailed. Twenty minutes later, she found to her surprise that she had been hired again, this time to be pressed into immediate service.

"Hi, I'm Sally Ryan, and I couldn't help overhearing," said her new co-worker, extending a hand when Annie reappeared from the rest room in waitress attire. "I'm something of a singer too. Are you new in town? You wouldn't by chance be looking for someone to share an apartment with?"

By the time Annie returned to the boardinghouse that evening, her feet felt as if they were encased in lead. But she had some earnings to her credit, plus the possibility of a more permanent place to live. As she climbed into bed, her gaze fell on Solange's white evening dress, which was hanging up to air in front of the open window.

The following morning she was scheduled to rehearse with Oscar, then present herself at the photographer's. Jake would be there, to make sure she looked right and posed the way he wanted her to. I'm going to snuff out this silly infatuation if it kills me, she thought, switching off the light. When I see him tomorrow, he won't have an inkling of how I feel.

Besides, I'm too tired to think about him tonight.

The photographer's studio was on the second floor of the Pontalba Apartments, facing the heart of the French Quarter, Jackson Square. Annie climbed the stairs carrying Solange's evening dress on a hanger swathed in plastic, her shoes and makeup packed in a small shoulder bag. As she walked into the outer office, she had misgivings she couldn't ignore. Exactly how did Jake plan to elicit the kind of portrait he wanted? she wondered. Would his siren-voiced secretary friend be aware of the tensions between them?

As if in answer to her question, a tall, curvaceous brunette in khaki trousers and an oversized silk designer shirt came out of the studio to greet her. For a moment, each appraised the other in silence. Annie sensed the kind of recognition that can take place between two women who are attracted to the same man.

Keeping her manner impersonal and tranquil, Annie introduced herself as she took inventory of the woman's short dark hair, vivid lipstick and cool air of confidence. So this is the kind of woman Jake is willing to romance, she thought. Definitely not the innocent type.

Then she was brought up sharply to attention. "I'm Yolande Carr," the other woman was saying. "The dressing room is right this way. Why not change and let me see what we have to work with? Jake should be along at any moment."

Annie couldn't help staring. "You're . . . the photographer?"

Her question evoked a lazy, brilliant smile. "What did you think? That this was solely a man's profession?"

"Not really. It's just that Jake never mentioned . . ."

Yolande gave a faint, elegant shrug. "How like him. Now, if you don't mind . . ."

I'm going, I'm going, Annie thought, actually quite grateful for the chance to disappear temporarily into the dressing room.

"Be sure to put on enough makeup," Yolande called after her. "The amount you're wearing now would be washed out completely by the lights."

As if I didn't know anything about stage makeup, Annie thought, grimacing at her reflection in the mirror. More than a little annoyed at the feeling that she'd been dismissed as an unlikely threat, she was determined to do well at the session. *And* put an end to any conclusion Yolande might have drawn that she was mad about Jake.

After taking off her street clothes, Annie fastened on the bare high-heeled sandals she'd bought less than an hour before, then slithered Solange's low-cut jersey gown over her shoulders and hips.

Makeup and hairdo in place, she emerged a few minutes later to find Jake waiting for her. A little flame leaped in his blue eyes as he looked her over from head to toe. "Lovely," he remarked, his voice faintly abrasive in that way she liked. Lightly he touched her shoulder, tested the feel of the fabric with his fingertips. "Just the sort of outfit I was hoping for."

"Sure it's cut low enough for you?" she jibed softly.

He let his gaze rest a moment too long on the dress's plunging neckline. "I didn't say *that*," he replied, giving her a wicked look. "Maybe I'm not willing to pay what it costs to sample the merchandise, but that doesn't mean I don't enjoy window shopping."

Furious, Annie stood there willing him to remove his touch. To her disgust, her pulse was racing again in that foolish way, her imagination ready to soar on one of its unreasoning flights.

As if he could read her mind, Jake dropped his hand. "Let's get started, 'Lande," he said casually. "Take a few warm-up shots, and we'll see how it goes."

"All right." Rolling up her pink silk sleeves, Yolande switched on her battery of strobe lights and adjusted them. "Stand here," she ordered, eyeing Annie with her head tilted to one side and then taking a light meter reading. A moment later, she was checking the settings on her camera. "Ready," she said.

To Annie's surprise, Jake handed her a mike. "This isn't live," he informed her, switching on a taped instrumental version of the song he'd chosen to play that first afternoon. "But I want you to sing into it as if you have a whole orchestra behind you."

From her position facing the glare of the strobes, the rest of the studio was nearly blotted out in shadow. But though she couldn't really see him, Jake's presence was a strong influence in the room, too strong to overcome as he rolled the tape back to the beginning and Yolande tripped the shutter on a few experimental frames.

To her chagrin and embarrassment, Annie's throat constricted, and her nails dug into her palms. She was freezing up, far more seriously than she had at the beginning of her audition two days before. "She's too stiff," she could hear Yolande complaining. "I won't be able to get a thing."

Jake gave a little shrug. "I'll see what I can do."

He turned off the tape recorder with a snap. "All right, Annie," he said, stepping closer, though his face remained in shadow. "Shut your eyes for a moment. Listen to me and don't think of anything else at all."

Sweating already from the heat of the lights, and half-angry, half-miserable, Annie complied.

"I want you to pretend it's just you and I, rehearsing together. That I'm playing the piano instead of a tape, waiting to hear you sing only for me. Okay?"

"Okay," she whispered.

"Now . . . start the song *a cappella,* and I'll bring up the music slowly."

Somehow, she managed to do as he asked. At first, her voice came out breathy and a little unsure. Then, as Jake started up the tape again, she caught hold and opened her eyes.

"That's the way, angel," he encouraged softly. "You're so damn beautiful you don't have to be shy. Don't pay any attention to the camera. Just sing it right to me."

Maybe it was the fact that she couldn't see him well there in the shadows. Or perhaps it was his voice, with a note she'd heard in it only once before, when he'd told her how very good she was to hold.

Whatever the reason, she let the song warm her and began moving about with the mike. Deliberately she tossed her hair so that it fell forward across her forehead in that exotic way he liked. If we were lovers, this is how it would be, she told him, weaving the unspoken message into the song's classic words. Every song I sang would be an invitation for you to do what we would both want so much.

"You've got it, baby."

Behind him, Yolande was whirring and clicking away, but Annie didn't hear that, at least not with her conscious mind.

"Use that gorgeous body," he was coaxing, half whispering, his voice low and full of promise. "Turn . . . *that's* it . . . Throw your head back and your hips forward, the way you did when you sang for Harry and me. Let your audience know how you feel about being a woman. Drive me crazy with what we both know you can give."

As if it were a dream sequence, Annie entered fully into the spirit of what he wanted. She let her feelings pour out in the torchy number he had chosen. As uneven as it had been before, her voice was now at its best, fully capable of wringing the last shred of emotion from every word.

Then, before she had quite realized it, they had finished. The orchestra started another tune, and Jake snapped off the tape. "That's it, Annie," he told her. "You were fantastic."

"I got some good ones, I think," Yolande was saying as she switched off the strobes. Clearly she was addressing her remarks to Jake. "I imagine you're in a hurry for them. They should be printed by four, if you want to stop back this afternoon."

Jake nodded. "How about some lunch?"

For a moment, Annie stood there blinking, her eyes momentarily unaccustomed to the absence of glaring light. Would Jake dismiss her so lightly then, after calling forth such a wellspring of emotion? And what did the sultry photographer think of the little game he had played with her? Probably that if she'd been taken in, she was a fool.

At the moment, Annie felt she had volunteered for the part. Bending over, she set the mike on the floor at her feet, then turned blindly away toward the dressing room.

"You're included in that invitation too," Jake called after her. "We'll probably just run over to the bakery for some soup and a sandwich."

Resolutely, she kept her back to him. "Thanks, but I can't," she told him, her voice as expressionless as she could make it. "I have another engagement."

5

~00000000000~

Annie's engagement, which she hadn't bothered to describe to Jake, was in fact that day's stint at the Jericho Oyster Bar. During the eight hours she spent on her feet, hustling food and drink for her customers, Annie didn't have much opportunity to reflect on the photography session. Still, she was left with a pervasive sense of embarrassment. She wasn't looking forward very much to signing the contract the following afternoon.

As she was leaving the studio, Jake had asked her to stop by his office for the signing. "Harry will be coming by to affix his John Henry too," he'd added.

She'd responded by letting him know she and Harry had already planned to come together. "I'm meeting him at the paper after I'm done with my morning rehearsal," she said, not explaining that Harry had invited her down for a look at the few clippings about her mother he'd been able to locate. The expression on Jake's face—a mixture of studied nonchalance and what might have been jealousy—had afforded her some small measure of retribution.

Tired as she was, she walked several blocks out of her way after work to inspect Sally Ryan's Royal Street apartment. To her surprise, she found its location delightful, if a little shabby and bizarre.

"Here we are!" Sally announced, motioning Annie to follow her through an arched entry and along a tunneled passage that nestled between an antique shop and a small art gallery. A number of bad paintings and several bicycles were piled helter-skelter against the passageway walls. A sign announced ZODIAC TEA ROOM —FORTUNES in faded letters.

At the far end of the passageway, a courtyard beckoned. Unlike Jake's, it wasn't very neatly kept. Just the same, Annie found herself smiling as her gaze rested on a weathered Cinzana umbrella, dilapidated straw chairs and potted plants of all descriptions and states of health. In the far right corner, Italian lights outlined the entrance to the palm reader's establishment. Vine tendrils curled along the second-floor balcony and climbed up the handrail of the worn stairway that led to Sally's abode. Bits of driftwood from some former tenant's art project were stacked on top of her air-conditioner.

"I like it," Annie responded to her new friend's questioning gaze.

Sally shrugged, though she was obviously pleased. "So do I," she said. "C'mon upstairs."

Though the tiny apartment, with its matchstick blinds, sagging couch upholstered in a faded cabbage-rose print, and two cubbyhole bedrooms, was anything but fancy, Annie didn't have to consider long before agreeing to move in and share rent with Sally when her paid-up week at the Oakleaf was over. At least I'll have a permanent address, a telephone number and something approximating a home, she thought.

But Annie had other things to worry about the following day as she arrived at the *Times-Picayune* Building. Even if it's going to be difficult working for Jake, I'm going to see this career thing through. I can't let myself freeze up again, with the opening only one day away.

Finding out about Solange was yet another reason to stay. I hope Harry found something, she thought—if only the tiniest clue.

Inside the building's two-story marble foyer, she gave her name to the receptionist and then waited while the woman phoned Harry in his second-floor office. "It's okay," the receptionist said with a smile as she put down the phone. "Go up the stairs and turn right, then right again once you're inside the newsroom. Harry Wilson's desk is in the far corner."

Annie located Harry in the sea of desks and video display terminals without much difficulty. "Well," he greeted her, getting to his feet and giving her a quick hug. "How's the practice with Oscar been going?"

"Pretty well, I think." She hesitated. "I have to admit it, though . . . I'm a little nervous about tomorrow night."

"Don't be." He indicated a chair. "And don't let Jake make you self-conscious, either. He won't be playing with the group for your opening, so you won't have to share the stage with him. Just pick a friendly face in the back of the room."

Is it that obvious to everyone that Jake throws me off-balance? she wondered as she sat down beside

Harry's littered desk. I'll have to get my emotions under better control. Then she forgot about Jake momentarily as Harry passed her several clippings about her mother, three of which she hadn't seen before.

First to catch her eye was an obituary accompanied by a postage-stamp-sized photograph. "Red Door Singer Dies After Brief Illness," its headline said. Matter-of-factly, the story gave the date of her mother's death and the place, a local hospital. Ned, Annie and the Trosclairs of Carteret were listed as survivors. I wonder why they included Ned's name when they were divorced? Annie thought, staring at the tiny photograph. Vainly she tried to see the young mother from Ned's snapshot in the ethereal blond singer with her huge, shadowed eyes.

"She was quite beautiful," Harry said, regarding her. "You look a lot like her, in case no one's ever told you."

"Thanks." Annie patted his hand. "I just hope I can live up to her talent."

"I suppose Jake played her record for you the other day."

"Yes, he did." And the less said about that, the better, she added to herself, turning over the second clipping in her hand. It was another review, very similar to the one Ned had saved for so many years.

A third news story described a brawl that had taken place at the club. Solange and the club's owner at the time, one Harold Dorsey, were quoted as witnesses.

"Dorsey's name is the only piece of new evidence I could turn up," Harry put in. "But I don't know how much help it's going to be. I checked him out in the city directory and a few other places. He may have died, or moved away. But according to official records, at least, he's no longer part of the New Orleans scene."

At Annie's request, Harry checked the directory

again, this time for some mention of her mother's landlady. The result was the same. "I'm afraid I'm not being much help," he said. "Let me buy your lunch instead."

After a quick bite in the newspaper's lunchroom, they drove downtown in Harry's sports car. Jake's office was on the twenty-first floor of a soaring modern building. The plaque on his door read JACOBSEN & ST. ARNOLD, A.I.A.

Moments later a middle-aged secretary was showing them into his office. "Come in, I've been expecting you," he said with that faintly lopsided smile that attracted her so much.

To Annie's dismay, he was even more handsome in business attire. To cover her reaction, she glanced quickly at her surroundings, taking in the large, light room with its bank of windows overlooking the city, his imposing desk, and drafting table littered with plans. With approval, she noted the paintings on his walls, the shelves of books, and the old jazz instruments he had used as wall ornaments. A healthy fiddle-leaf fig sat in a brass planter.

Though the office was quite different in style and tone from Paradise Lost and the offbeat, artistic apartment situated above its courtyard, she had to admit that it, too, seemed well suited to his personality.

"Won't you all sit down?" he asked, waving her and Harry to a pair of aubergine velvet chairs that contrasted beautifully with the pale gray walls and dove-colored carpet. "May I fix you a drink while you go over the contract?"

"Can't, I'm working," mumbled Harry as he went over the details of the document in his rapid, analytical fashion. "Looks okay to me. Got a pen handy?"

"How about you, Annie?" asked Jake as he handed his partner a slim black fountain pen ornamented with his initials in gold. "I've got the makings of a gin and tonic if that would suit you."

She refused to be flattered that he had remembered. "No, thanks," she said. "This is business. We celebrated the other day, remember?"

It was an unfortunate choice of words. Not only had she reminded him of the drinks the three of them had shared at the bar, but also of the painful little scene à deux that had followed in his apartment. To avoid the memory she saw in his eyes, Annie took the contract Harry was handing her and hastily scanned its contents.

"It states what we agreed, as far as I can tell," she acknowledged, scrawling her signature in quadruplicate as well. "If you're leaving right away, Harry, I'd appreciate a ride."

"As a matter of fact, I am. I've got a six p.m. deadline on my weekender piece."

They both got to their feet. "I can take you back to the Quarter, Annie, if you like," Jake said, looking from her to his partner and back again. "I have to go anyway, and it's off Harry's route. Besides, if you have a minute, there's something I'd like to discuss with you."

She frowned. "Won't it wait?"

"I suppose it could. But I'd rather we got this out of the way, with the opening coming up tomorrow."

"All right, then." Wishing Harry goodbye, she walked over to the window and stood with her back to the room while he and Jake had a few parting words. Then she heard the door close, felt Jake come to stand behind her.

"I want to apologize," he said in that deep, faintly rough voice of his.

"What for this time?" She gazed out resolutely at the Mississippi River Bridge, while inwardly she winced at her own sarcastic tone.

"For the way I behaved at my apartment. And for embarrassing you at the studio the other day. I honestly didn't mean to do that."

She shrugged. "Forget it."

"I'd rather you forgave me. It might please you to know that the pictures we got were worth the anguish. Stunning is the way I'd describe them, for lack of a better word."

Annie didn't bite, though she was sorely tempted. Even if I look like the most glamorous thing since Billie Holiday with her gardenia, she vowed, I'm going to wait until he volunteers to show them to me himself.

But he didn't offer, at least not right away. "I have a present for you, one I was hoping would help me make amends," he said softly instead.

She turned to face him at that. "Don't imagine I'd accept anything—"

"You can accept this."

Picking up Solange's record from his desk, he held it out to her. "I planned to give you this the other day," he said. "You should be the one to have it, whether or not you decide we can be friends."

Annie took the record with trembling fingers. She felt as if a tiny piece of the heritage she'd missed for so long had finally come back into her possession. "Thank you . . . very much," she whispered. "I *would* like . . . to be friends with you."

"Then it's settled." Not laying a hand on her, he leaned over and lightly kissed her cheek. "You really are something of an angel in this day and age, you know," he said. "Just the way your mother was in hers."

Vigorously Annie shook her head. "No," she said. "That's wrong. Solange was no angel, and neither am I."

Jake gave her a disbelieving smile. "Sorry," he said. "But that's how I see you. I'm surprised you haven't seen the ad yet. It was in this morning's paper."

A half hour later he was handing her out of his sleek black Corvette at the Oakleaf Residence, a copy of the ad folded in her pocket. "Hot jazz and Cajun laments by Miss Annie Duprez, Bayou Angel," it stated in bold typography. It was hard for her to believe that the scintillating and uninhibited singer in the photograph was actually the Annie she knew.

Tensions didn't abate for her that evening, as she worked a four-hour shift at the Jericho. Nor did she relax very much when later she fell into a restless, dream-filled slumber. "You're a bundle of nerves, girl," Oscar told her the next morning when she showed up for their final practice session before the opening. "Better slow down and take it as it comes."

Fortunately, Jake was nowhere to be seen. "I'm trying," she told the avuncular piano player with a halfhearted smile as she stepped up to the mike. "But it's a big responsibility. That ad in the paper . . . I don't want to make Jake or Harry look like a fool."

"Hell, you won' do that, honey." Oscar grinned, then patted the piano keys to produce a few inviting phrases. "Jus' let the music calm you," he advised. "That's where you live, in case you don't remember."

To her surprise, Oscar's advice seemed to have some effect. When she walked back to the Oakleaf at about one-thirty to take a nap, she felt for the first time that she had her repertoire firmly in hand. Still she was keyed up and more than a little nervous when she arrived back at the club at a quarter after seven, carrying the freshly cleaned strapless black velvet gown in its garment bag.

The warm-up group was playing, and already there were quite a few people sitting at the club's little round tables as she went in through the courtyard entrance. Jake still wasn't in evidence. Spotting her almost immediately, Harry led her back to the small dressing room he and Jake had fixed up next to the office they shared.

"My partner's been detained," he supplied, apparently noting her sidelong glances and guessing their object. "The client for his Florida Centre project is in town. He'll probably make it just in time for your opening."

She was scheduled to start at eight. Strains of old jazz staples floated across the courtyard as she dressed and applied her makeup with a careful if slightly unsteady hand.

I don't know why it should matter, she thought, looking into the mirror when she'd finished. But there's no denying it. You chose this dress because it gives the lie to Jake's theory that you're such an angel.

Just then there was a short rap on the dressing room door. "Are you decent?" Jake's voice called.

"Yes," she said. A little shiver ran along her back-bone. "Come in."

He opened the door and stepped inside, rakish in his snowy evening shirt and perfectly tailored black dinner jacket and trousers. The two of them were impossibly cramped in the small space.

"Annie, my God, but you're beautiful," he breathed.

"That dress . . . your skin is like milk. They're going to eat their hearts out."

The admiration in his words was reflected in those light, beautiful eyes that so easily showed his thoughts. Any possible reply stuck in her throat.

Jake seemed to catch himself, working to get his thoughts and emotions under better control. "Say something," he added with a hint of his usual teasing manner. "Prove to me the cat hasn't got your tongue. I want to be sure you'll be able to sing when you step into the spotlight."

"Don't worry," she managed. "I'm all right. With Oscar up there, I'm going to be fine."

"Good. I suppose Harry told you . . . he's arranged for a substitute critic to cover us; I understand he's already in the audience. My aunt and uncle are here too. And one of my biggest clients, who turns out to be a jazz buff happened to be in town and tagged along tonight."

Doubtless Jake didn't realize that his comments weren't exactly calculated to instill confidence. How like a man, she thought—somewhat fondly in spite of herself. But it didn't really matter whom he wanted her to impress, because she knew she was going to be okay. "They won't know what hit them," she told him.

He nodded, and his expression seemed to soften. "You have the same effect on me, Annie," he said.

Somehow, without her quite knowing how it had happened, Jake's strong arms were coming around her, his mouth descending on hers. But he didn't ravage it this time. Instead he kissed her gently, with the greatest of tenderness, as if she were someone special, to cherish and protect.

Oh, there were passionate undertones too, no mistaking them—fiery hidden currents that she knew could blaze up at the slightest provocation. At the moment, though, he wasn't allowing them free expression. Surrendering, she just stood there, giving herself over to the feeling of being held in his arms.

Finally, he drew back a little, his hands still warm on her shoulders. He didn't seem sorry about what he'd done this time—not sorry at all.

"Jake . . . ," she began.

He shook his head. With the corner of his handkerchief, he carefully removed a bit of lipstick he'd smudged. "I didn't mean to change the rules without consulting you," he murmured. "Let's just say that kiss was for luck. I wish you the best."

The excitement and longing Jake had brought to the surface stayed with her as they walked across the courtyard together. Annie could see that the hands on the clock over the club's Bourbon Street entrance stood at five minutes to the hour. The warm-up group had departed, and now the musicians she'd heard that first afternoon were taking their places on the bandstand. A skinny black youth with an enormous smile was sitting in Jake's place. Oscar, who would lead the quintet tonight, was glancing at the back door, looking for her.

"They're going to play a couple of numbers first to massage the crowd," Jake said into her ear. "We'll wait out here. When Oscar tells me it's time, I'll introduce you, call you up to the mike."

"Okay."

He squeezed her hand.

Later, she was unable to say just what songs had been played, or what jokes Oscar had told to establish rapport with the audience. The place had filled up while she'd been in the dressing room, and she realized she would be singing to a full house. A number of people were in evening dress—Jake's and Harry's relatives, friends and business associates, she guessed. There had been some mention of a party afterward. I have to do well, she reminded herself, the nervousness beginning again.

In the end, it was easier than she'd guessed. Giving her hand another squeeze, Jake went in at Oscar's signal and said some complimentary things that made her blush, though later she couldn't remember what they were. Then she was walking toward the bandstand to a friendly round of applause, her obvious shyness in direct contrast to the daring, strapless gown.

For a moment, the glare of the lights blinded her. But she didn't hesitate. Oscar had decided she should begin her first set on a fast, upbeat note to please the crowd. Now, as he gave her the opening bars of an old Helen O'Connell favorite, she plunged in with everything she had. As if by some instantaneous chemical reaction, her shyness evaporated and all the brilliant, swinging clarity she was capable of came into play.

Waves of applause met her at the finish, and she bowed low, trusting that the bodice of her dress would hold as she murmured her thanks and included the members of the quintet in the honors.

No fear was left in her as she unclipped the mike to move about in front of the musicians and talk to her audience, telling them how long she had wanted to sing there, on the stage where once her mother had stood.

She could feel them loving it—loving that she had taken them into her confidence, and loving her music. Carried away by their approval and affection, she used her body with confidence and her voice to its fullest range.

Until that moment, she hadn't sung specifically to his table. She knew where he was sitting, to the right of the stage with a graying, urbane-looking man she guessed must be his client, and an older couple who were probably his uncle and aunt. Though she'd half expected Yolande Carr to join the party, the brunette photographer hadn't put in an appearance.

Now she dared to sing for him, veering away from the intensity of his gaze only when it became apparent something was happening between them that was too private for the eyes of strangers.

She ended by directing the last verse at Harry, who was seated with some friends at the opposite side of the room. Not waiting for the applause to die, she moved as Oscar had instructed into her last number of the set, a frenetic and sizzling scat vocalization.

"Leave the folks wantin' more," the piano player had advised her. "Make 'em sorry the set has to end."

The applause was deafening as she bowed, fastened the mike back in its stand and stepped down from the stage. To her astonishment, the musicians themselves were clapping too. People were crowding around, but somehow she wasn't surprised at all when Jake deftly removed her from the melee and settled her at his table.

Champagne and introductions were waiting, along with Harry, who had come over to bestow a brotherly kiss.

"That was extraordinary, my dear," said the elegant, motherly woman who was introduced as Bethia Jacobsen, Jake's aunt by marriage and the wife of his architectural partner.

"I heartily second that, young lady." The compliment had come from Stephen Morel, Jake's client from St.

Petersburg. "I'm sure the great Ella would approve of your interpretation on that last number."

Instinctively she looked at Jake. *We have a lot to talk about,* his eyes communicated over the rim of his champagne glass. *When we're alone.* "I agree, it was spectacular," he said aloud. "You gave one classy performance, angel."

From that moment forward, the evening seemed to dissolve into one shimmering amalgam of music and applause and heady, sparkling wine. Between sets, when the quintet played without her or took a much-deserved break, Jake was never far from her side— refilling her glass and then teasing her that she'd had enough, resting one arm across the back of her chair while he gestured to his friends to make a point.

She could feel Harry's level gaze on them, and she knew he must be wondering what had happened to change things between them. At the moment, though, it didn't matter to her what Harry thought. I'm a little giddy from the champagne, she decided, aware she was glowing at full wattage and far more talkative than usual. In truth, she was drunk with the music and applause . . . and more than a little drunk on Jake.

Onstage, she knew, she was giving the performance of her life. Her interaction with the audience was like a love affair. Clamoring for more, her listeners pushed Annie into giving from the deepest part of herself, even while she was greedy for their adulation.

For the first time, she knew what it was to be beyond fatigue, to sing and sing and never tire, mixing jazz with blues and scat vocals, then hushing the house with the unexpected innocence of her Cajun songs.

Her eyes were glittering and her emotions perilously

near the surface when Jake finally declared the club closed at three a.m. and announced to his invited guests that the *real* party was just getting under way.

Balancing a rum and Coke in one hand, Oscar threw his arms around her in an affectionate, congratulatory hug, then returned to the bandstand to play some more tunes—this time with several guests who had brought their own instruments along for a jam session. To Annie's surprise, white-uniformed waiters wheeled in a sumptuous buffet through the courtyard entrance, then uncorked more champagne and passed it among the guests.

While first Harry and then Stephen Morel escorted her onto the dance floor, Jake allowed himself to be lured up to the drummer's chair. Though at first he offered the group nothing more than background accompaniment, she could feel the subtle yet distinctive change in rhythmic style he brought to the music. It didn't escape her notice, either, the way those little lines about his mouth curved with amusement and satisfaction as he watched her dancing with Morel.

On the next number, Jake was persuaded to play a solo. For the second time, he made Annie think of Buddy Rich. To her, his playing had the same driving, pounding undercurrents and almost melodic highlights that set the great drummer and bandleader apart. Everyone stopped dancing, and she was free to watch, to drink in the way he made light careen off the cymbals, drumsticks blur in his agile fingers. She might have been his lover the way she gazed at him, striving to preserve in memory the look of his loosened tie and open shirt collar, the little rivulets of perspiration that gleamed against his skin, his frown of total concentration.

Then it was over. Jake was mopping his brow, everyone was applauding, and he was smiling that faintly crooked smile. Jimmy Darnell, the young drummer who had accompanied Annie's singing, was patting him on the back and resuming his place on the bandstand.

A moment later Jake had returned to her side. Tossing his jacket over a chair, he reached for Annie's hand and drew her gently to him. There was a heart-stopping message in his beautiful eyes. "It's time we danced together, my beautiful Miss Duprez," he told her softly and insistently. "Rules or no rules, I don't intend doing without you tonight."

6

Heedless of who might have overheard his comments, Jake enfolded her in his arms. They began to move to the music, dancing so close that they were just a breath apart. Of course, he was a consummate dancer; somehow she'd known he would be. Smoothly, effortlessly, gracefully, he led her with greater mastery and timing than she had ever known. His lean fingers, pressed against the small of her back through the velvet gown, guided her every step, making her feel cherished and featherlight, though she was imprisoned tightly in his arms.

How I've longed for just such a chance to hold him, she thought, feeling the combined aromas of cigarette smoke, aftershave and his distinctive skin scent enveloping her.

But she had to admit it—more than anything, his

words and their blatant implication had set her imagination racing. Did he really mean what I imagine he did? she wondered. Or will he change his mind again and say he wants me to go?

As if he sensed her uncertainty, Jake tugged her even more closely against him, so that she was molded to intimate knowledge of his body. There could no doubt how much he wanted her. At the piano, like a guardian angel, Oscar switched to something slow, sensuous and full of feeling. The rippling cascades and occasional blue notes were perfectly patterned for a man and woman moving together, discovering the tactile pleasures of being in each other's arms.

A man and woman falling hard for each other, she amended, half-wild with wanting him. Because that's what's happening, at least to me.

"Annie?" he said. There was a testing quality in the single word that she couldn't mistake.

"I'm here," she told him, her head buzzing with excitement and champagne.

Somehow it was the answer he required. "I know you are," he whispered, tucking her right hand against his chest and putting both arms around her, leaning his cheek sweetly against her hair. Intuitively she knew it was a gesture of surrender, a sign of willingness, for that night at least, to break their self-imposed rules and have what they both wanted.

From that moment on, they danced only with each other, their longing only made sharper by a brassy, bluesy trumpet solo, Jimmy Darnell's insistent heartbeat on the drums, Oscar's suggestive whole-note pauses. Even when they took a break from the dance floor, they were inseparable. Jake held tightly and possessively to her hand, as if he didn't want to let go of her even for a moment. She knew their behavior left no doubt in anyone's mind: they had become a couple, publicly burning with an intense and private desire.

Finally, at nearly four-thirty, they were bidding the last of their guests good night.

"It's been such a pleasure meeting you, Annie," Jake's aunt told her warmly, giving her a curious and somehow approving look from behind gold-rimmed glasses. "You have extraordinary talent, my dear, in case you don't realize it. My husband and I would be delighted to have you as our guest at a birthday dinner he's throwing in my honor." She named a date and an address, which she added could be found in the Garden District.

Annie looked at Jake. "I'll see to it she gets there, Aunt Bethia," he said, giving the name its long-voweled, Southern pronunciation.

Then everyone had gone except for Oscar, Harry and the two of them. After switching off the lights and sound equipment, Oscar saluted them as he ambled off to his own quarters to check on his grandson. With an air of restraint, Harry clapped Jake lightly on the shoulder, gave Annie a shy little kiss. For a moment, the two men's eyes met and held in a man-to-man communication that only they fully understood.

"I'll only be a minute," Jake murmured when his partner had gone. Leaving Annie standing in the middle of the darkened dance floor, which was lit now only by the exit lights, he locked the street doors and picked up the cash drawer.

With his dinner jacket slung over one shoulder, he returned to her side. "Ready, darling?" he asked with a little catch in his lovely, rough voice, as if this time were different, no matter how many women he'd invited upstairs in the past.

She nodded, and he led her out into the courtyard, locking the back door behind them. He put one arm around her, and they walked across the courtyard, turning off the fountain as they went. Then they were climbing the narrow iron-railed stairs as they had only a few short days before.

It's really going to happen this time, Annie thought, a little feverish at the notion. I'll know what it's like to feel the totality of his passion—fall asleep afterward in his arms.

Jake's apartment looked different by the glow of a single lamp. *"Chez moi, chez toi,"* he said softly, putting down his jacket and the cash box and taking her lightly in his arms.

Keenly aware that they were alone now, that whatever they wanted to happen between them could happen, Annie stepped out of her shoes and kicked them aside. Slipping her own arms about his neck, she mutely offered up her mouth.

He accepted it this time as if there could be no turning aside. "My God, how I've wanted you," he admitted, covering it with blunt little kisses she thought would sear her very soul. Then he was entering with his tongue, invading her moist recesses as if in imitation of the act of love. She moaned a little at the sensation of his hands, so swiftly moving to her breasts, pushing down the bodice of her velvet gown.

A moment later, Jake was on his knees, turning her a little toward the light the better to see the ripe fullness he had revealed as he cupped it in his hands. Tenderly, he pressed against her nipples, exciting them with his thumbs. She could feel her breasts firm and swell, as if she were woman incarnate.

Then his mouth was on her and she lost all reason, swaying slightly as he caressed each nipple in turn, to suck at it wetly and flick it from side to side with his tongue. Hot currents ran from Annie's breasts to her innermost reaches. Fiercely she drew his dark head against her, inviting—no, demanding—that he push and tug at her with greater abandon.

Never had a man promised such release, such glory. With him I have no shame, she exulted as he got to his feet again, his hands straying from her breasts to the zipper catch on her dress. I want him to leave no part of me untouched, to take me and fill me with everything he has to give.

Even so, she gave a little gasp at the expert way he stripped off her gown, so easily that seconds later it was a velvet pool about her ankles. Throbbing with pride at the way he was staring at the result of his handiwork, she stepped free, allowing him to remove her panty hose and tiny wisp of an undergarment.

"Skin like satin," he muttered thickly, still fully clothed in his evening trousers and half-open shirt as he ran his hands over her body's ripe curves and tender hollows.

This was a man who wouldn't stand on any conventions of modesty, she realized seconds later, flinching with pleasure as he found the very core of her desire.

"Jake, please . . ." Her voice came out ragged gulps as the sensation became unbearably sweet, making it seem as if her throat too swollen with wanting. "Take off your things. Please . . . I want you . . ."

"We'll be more comfortable in my bed." His own

words gruff with desire, he swept her up into his arms, carried her up the spiral staircase.

His big, high-ceilinged bedroom was lost in shadow. He settled her against smooth bed pillows and placed a devouring little kiss on her mouth, then tore himself away momentarily to open the dark wood shutters that covered the room's tall, arching windows. Above the ancient rooftops of the Quarter, she could see that a few lights still burned in the city's skyscrapers, set sparingly against their shadowy shapes like diamonds. The buildings loomed over the low houses of the Quarter, creating a surreal juxtaposition of new and old that was touching and beautiful.

In the faint moonlight, she could also make out a little of the room—a gauzy white canopy over the heavy bamboo four-poster, the overhead shape of a ceiling fan, an armoire bulking in the shadows. He had come to stand again beside the bed, looking silently down at her.

For a second, perhaps, she read both hunger and reluctance in his eyes. "Jake?" she questioned, wondering at his ambivalence.

Without responding, he traced the length of her slowly with his finger from the tip of her nose, over parted lips, both upturned breasts and her taut mound of belly, stopping at one foot's sensitive sole. "You're so damn beautiful it hurts to look at you," he told her with a little shake of his head.

"Then don't just look." Restless against the sheets, she held out her hands to him. "Take off your things."

"Whatever you say, sweetheart."

His hands went to his collar, jerking loose his tie and tossing it to the floor. Never taking his eyes from her, he unbuttoned and shrugged off his shirt, revealing the dark furring of body hair that covered his arms and chest. Annie thought she would die of wanting to tangle her fingers in it, longing to help as he tugged at the buckle of his belt and then unzipped his trousers.

He was wearing nothing underneath. She gave a sharp intake of breath even as her eyes devoured his flat stomach, narrow hips and thighs, his male desire eager and ready for her.

"Darling," she pleaded hoarsely, leaving all but that one word of her demand unspoken.

"Not yet." Lying down on the bed beside her, he pressed the length of his body against hers. "I want to please you, baby," he whispered, his knowing hands and mouth already doing their work. "Make you wild."

Annie knew she would never forget what it was like to lie in Jake's arms that night, a willing prisoner of his expert ministrations. For her, it was as if a new world had opened, one unexpectedly wild and delicious in the texture and magnitude of its pleasures. With his loving finesse—and perhaps, more simply, with the fact of who he was—he pushed her far beyond what she had imagined possible, setting her adrift from every mooring of control.

Good as his word, he used his obvious experience to bring her to a quivering brink of readiness again and again, postponing his own gratification. Overwhelmed by the need he was evoking, and aroused almost as much by his outrageous whispers of lust and praise, Annie gave herself over entirely to the dangers of the moment. Too easily she forgot her determination not to give hostages to fortune, or how difficult it might be to walk away later if she learned to care too much.

Instead, she opened her heart to Jake along with her

body, giving to him without reservation. For she knew it now: *he* was the unconventional, sensuous man she had dreamed about all those years in Houma when her father had hinted repeatedly that she should settle down.

His was the dark head she had longed for at her breast, his the mouth she had ached to have trace a burning path down her body, bringing her to a precipice of pleasure again and again, only to quiet her a little and make it last.

His the hard legs she had dreamed would push her own smooth thighs apart, demanding access even as he was demanding it now. Yet still he didn't move inside to claim her.

Suddenly she was raging, incandescent to have him on her own terms, the same consummate terms he was insisting of her. She wanted him to want her in the same absolute way, so desperately that he couldn't wait, that he would move like an avalanche to cover her. All inhibition flown, she dared to touch him as he was touching her, to seek for and caress his male desire, draw him toward her emptiness.

"Do that," he growled, his voice shaky with surprise and pleasure, "and we'll soon end this, angel."

Annie shook her head, her hair spread out against the pillow. "I don't care," she told him, her own words blurring with emotion. "I want to feel you . . . crashing into me . . . This needn't be the last time we have each other . . . only the first . . ."

Clearly her words had struck an erotic nerve. Murmuring of his desire to have her again and again until they both dropped from exhaustion, he moved over her and thrust deeply within. His presence there nearly touched off a cataclysm of rapture. For a moment, he didn't move, obviously struggling to maintain a self-command he had nearly lost.

Now I know what it is to be connected to the universe, Annie thought, when finally he began to move again, prompting her to an answering rhythm that was as ancient as womankind. In some half-cognizant way, she realized she truly *had* Jake now, possessed the driving, pounding essence of who he was.

He'd predicted correctly that it couldn't last. Washing over them, the waves of pleasure they made together had ever more towering peaks. Unable to help themselves, they gave way at almost the same moment, breaking free in mutual shudders of delight that reached from head to toe.

With a groan, Jake collapsed against her, pressing her deep into the luxurious comfort of his mattress, his body heavy and prickled with gooseflesh in her arms. Lovingly she held him, even as her own skin shivered delicately in response. A deep ache of satisfaction spread outward to her thighs, enveloping her in a delicious lethargy of contentment.

How I love you, Jake, she told him silently, as the heat spread through her body, causing a warm flush to surface on her cheeks. I didn't want to, and I imagine I'm going to regret it later. But I can't help it. And I wouldn't want to be anywhere else in the world tonight.

In truth, it had long been Sunday morning. First light was diffusing through the windows as, thoroughly kissed and cherished, she curled to sleep in his arms. Church bells from distant St. Louis Cathedral were faint on the air when she stirred sometime later under the white pima coverlet. Only a glimmer of full sunlight penetrated the room; Jake had apparently closed the dark wooden shutters again while she slept. Temporarily disoriented, she experienced a momentary sense of loss when she discovered the bed was empty of him.

Then she saw him, wearing just his khaki shorts and sitting in a rattan and leather chair, smoking and drinking coffee and watching her. Delicious scents from a silver pot and a napkin-covered plate on the little table beside him assailed her nostrils. He had retrieved her velvet gown from the living room and hung it from the armoire. Her panty hose and underwear had been neatly folded and placed at the foot of the bed.

Coming fully awake, she sensed it immediately: something was wrong. He didn't get up, didn't move toward the bed to take her in his arms. It struck her with force that there would be no morning lovemaking along with the croissants and coffee, perhaps not even a good-morning kiss.

"Well," he said, his blue eyes narrowing a little, "so you're finally awake. It's after eleven in the morning, you know. I suppose you'll want to borrow a robe to sit up and drink your coffee."

His distant, businesslike tone was unmistakable. She got the firm but unhappy impression she wouldn't be staying long. Probably he was only following the letter of social convention in such situations, providing breakfast before nudging her out the door. *He was right and I was wrong,* she thought miserably. *That was the last time we'll ever make love. I should have let him draw it out forever.*

"Say something," he prompted. A muscle twitched alongside his mouth, though there was no humor in his eyes. "Do you want me to hand you a robe, or would you prefer your gown?"

How terribly romantic you are this morning, Jake St. Arnold, she thought, unable to keep from feeling a little ashamed and bitter.

"Neither," she snapped, unable to keep a faint edge of sarcasm from her voice. "I always breakfast in the nude."

His eyes came fully open at that, with a glimmer of interest in them that she preferred not to acknowledge under the circumstances.

In response, she attempted a laugh. "Got you," she said. "Actually, I'd appreciate the robe. My street clothes are downstairs in the dressing room. But I want a shower before I have my coffee."

For Annie, the warm spray in his white-tiled shower stall was cathartic, a replacement for tears. You did what you wanted to do, and now you must pay the price, she reminded herself, drying off with one of his thick beige towels. Never mind that you love him now. You're a big girl, and you'll go on working for him, keep things on a friendly basis. You knew in your heart last night that part of him didn't want this to happen, that you helped him silence that inner objection, trapped him with his own sexual need.

She was noncommittal as she came back out wrapped in a cotton robe that was much too big for her. While she'd been occupied in the bath, she noted, he had fetched her things and placed them on the bed beside her underwear.

Not making more than a perfunctory attempt at conversation, she took the companion chair to his and helped herself to a croissant. I'll be cool about this if it kills me, she thought, sipping at his strong, chicory-flavored coffee while he scanned the Sunday paper.

As soon as she could possibly do so without losing her composure, she would get to her feet and announce her departure. But when she did, something in his attitude seemed to change. "Annie, wait," he said, getting up and settling his hands on her shoulders. "We should talk . . ."

Right now, the last thing she wanted was for him to touch her. Lightly she stepped aside, giving him a bright, impersonal smile. If a one-night stand is what you wanted, you got it, she thought. "I really have to get back and change, you know," she told him. "I have to report to work this afternoon."

Jake's face took on an air of bafflement. "But the club's closed today . . . it's Sunday," he began.

Disappointed and embarrassed as she was, she couldn't help feeling some wry amusement. "I know that," she replied with exaggerated patience as she picked up her things and headed back to the bathroom. "I'm sure you realize that my job at Paradise Lost doesn't pay me enough to live on. I'm a part-time waitress at the Jericho Oyster Bar." Without giving him a chance to respond, Annie turned and closed the bathroom door behind her.

After she had dressed, Jake insisted on driving her home. As they pulled up at the boardinghouse, she had the irrational notion that, after all this, he was thinking of kissing her goodbye.

"See you on Wednesday night," she told him airily, forestalling any such possibility as she got out of the car with only the briefest of backward looks. "I may come by some morning to practice with Oscar before then."

With a perplexed look on his face, as if he weren't certain which of them had retreated with the greater haste from their liaison of the night before, Jake opened his mouth as if to stop her. But, "Goodbye then, Annie," was all he said.

That afternoon before going to work, Annie moved her few possessions to Sally's apartment. Afterward, the two of them walked to the oyster house together.

"That was some review about you in the paper," Sally commented as they strolled. "I'd love to get praise for my singing like that someday."

"Review?" Annie looked at her new friend in astonishment. "Jake didn't say anything . . ."

Sally's brows rose slightly. "I guess you must have been reading the paper with your boss this morning," she replied, much too quick on the uptake.

Annie flushed. "Not exactly," she demurred, then shook her head. Why hide it? "You might as well know . . . Jake and I spent the night together," she said. "It isn't going to happen again. And he *was* looking at the entertainment section this morning, though I was too wrapped up in what was happening between us . . . or *not* happening . . . to think about a review. I wonder why he didn't call it to my attention."

Sally shrugged as they reached their place of employment. "Who knows?" she said with a flip little smile that expressed volumes. "Maybe he was having similar thoughts. I never could understand men anyway."

To her surprise, Annie was something of a celebrity at the little seafood café and bar. Customers who recognized her from the review promised to come by and catch her show. Even Bubba, who at his best never seemed to be gregarious, made a fuss about having a famous singer in his establishment.

Like the work, the praise did her ego good and

distracted her from thinking too much about Jake. Only when she was alone in her new bedroom at Sally's that night did the emotional pain of what had happened become real. Lying between Sally's best muslin sheets, she ached for his hands on her body, the sweet, marauding kisses of his mouth. *It was so good between us*, she agonized, tears finally slipping out to dampen the pillowcase. *Better than good.*

I'd be the last woman to try to saddle him with permanence. Why doesn't he want to want me?

7

At the club on Wednesday night, Jake was like a stranger. Indeed, he was behaving quite as if she'd been the one to draw back first from any further involvement. During the breaks, it was Harry who got her a cola from the bar and pulled out a chair for her at his table. Being a reporter, Jake's partner was full of questions, she guessed. But he was too much of a gentleman to ask them, probably because of the highly personal nature of the situation.

Certain now that her relationship with Jake would be strictly business in the future, Annie was more than a little surprised Thursday afternoon to find his message waiting for her at the restaurant. "Harry told me you were looking for a man named Harold Dorsey," he'd scrawled in his confident hand. "I've checked around and I know where you can find him. But it's not the sort of place you should visit alone."

Giving her the name and address of a Bourbon Street club that she didn't recognize, he'd added the single initial "J" in lieu of a signature. Maybe he doesn't want me for his lover, she thought. And maybe he has his reasons. But I was wrong to think he doesn't care.

Her excitement at having a new avenue to explore on her search into her mother's past was only enhanced by the notion that, once again, Jake had taken a hand in her affairs.

On Friday afternoon, long before it was time to get ready for the evening's performance, she hung Solange's silver and blue bugle-bead-encrusted gown in the Paradise Lost dressing room and walked east on Bourbon looking for the Three Star Lounge. Several blocks later she found it, a small quonset-roofed building tucked between two larger establishments. A dirty awning framed its entrance, and pictures of nude women were plastered across its windows. No wonder I didn't really notice it before, she thought, peering into the tiny, X-rated bistro through its partially open doorway.

An older man she might have taken for a vagrant, with the bulging stomach and red, vein-mottled face of an alcoholic, was sweeping up the sidewalk. Earning a few dollars for his next bottle, she thought with combined pity and distaste.

"Excuse me," she ventured, raising her voice a little. "Do you know if the manager's about?"

The man fixed her with his bleary gaze. "If you're lookin' for a job, you can ask the bouncer. We're short one bimbo in here tonight." Using a few choice anatomical words to describe her qualifications for the position of exotic dancer, he added, "Name's Steve. He'll be in around six."

"I . . . don't want a job." Annie retreated a little from the man's sour breath and even more rancid disposition. "Actually, I'm looking for someone named Harold Dorsey. He *is* the manager of this place, isn't he?"

With a short, ironic laugh, the man shook his head. "I'm Dorsey," he said. "Should I know you, lady?"

Taken aback for a moment, she found it was her turn to stare. *This* was the man who had known her mother, played Jake to her Annie at the old Red Door?

Looking at him now, it was impossible to imagine her delicate blond mother in his arms. "You . . . knew my mother," she stammered, sick at heart.

"Hey, maybe you do look familiar." Removing his torn and threadbare cap, Dorsey scratched his head, then squinted at her appraisingly. "What did you say her name was?"

Maybe some secrets are better left untold, she thought, uncertain now whether she wanted him to remember. But unlikely though he was, this foul-mouthed, hard-as-nails old man was her only lead. "Solange Duprez," she confessed, feeling like a traitor to her mother's memory. "She was a singer at the old Red Door years ago when you were the manager there."

Harold Dorsey's features took on a nostalgic look, then darkened. "The Frenchie," he said, his tone one of disgust. "Yeah. I remember her."

Annie was almost afraid to pursue the subject further. "What . . . was she like?" she asked hesitantly. "You see, I never knew her."

"That so? Then you ain't the little brat she always had hangin' around with her. The one whose daddy came to get her with a court order, took her out of that den of sin."

Annie's mind was spinning. "You say she had a child," she said slowly. "But I thought—"

"You want to know what I thought of her?" Dorsey interrupted. "Well, I'll tell you. She was a snob . . . too good for the rest of us. She had her fancy boyfriends, from the Garden District all the way out to Carrollton."

Annie winced, then plunged ahead, unwilling to run from the truth now just because it might be unpleasant to face. "Were there many?" she asked in a small voice. "Boyfriends, that is?"

Dorsey gave her an appraising look, seeming to read on her face which answer she didn't want to hear. "Hell, yes," he said with satisfaction. "There was a different one after her every night, even if she *was* still married to her poor sap of a husband."

Her eyes stinging with unshed tears, Annie turned away, stumbling a little in her haste on the uneven pavement. Dear God, she thought. It's even worse than I'd feared. No wonder Ned wouldn't talk about her, or cash the bank drafts she sent.

With heartfelt determination, she vowed again that she'd never follow in Solange's footsteps and take on a husband and a child only to abandon them and ruin their lives. Yet even as she shuddered at the picture Harold Dorsey had painted, a new thought entered her mind. At least my mother loved me enough to bring me with her, Annie realized, feeling the first inroads of comfort into her heart.

Unconsciously, she slowed her pace as the idea took hold. It was several hours yet until she had to think about getting ready for the show. For the moment, at least, she was free to stroll in the sunlight while she attempted to make sense of what she'd learned.

An hour or so later, Annie found herself back on the

sidewalk outside Paradise Lost. Standing with the crowd listening to the afternoon group play, she watched the neighborhood kids break dance on the sidewalk for tips. All of the boys were older than Dabney Washington, but not that much older, she realized. How would it have been, she wondered, if I had grown up here? Probably not the same as it will be for Dabney. In Oscar, he has somebody special to look after him.

Rounding the corner of the building, she ran into the boy himself. Looking a bit lonely, Oscar's grandson was drawing an uneven hopscotch diagram on the pavement.

"What's going on here, Dabney?" she asked with a smile. "I thought your grandpa was taking you out to the park this afternoon."

Dabney shrugged his narrow shoulders. "He took sick, Miss Annie," he explained. "It's his gall bladder again. You know how to play hopscotch?"

As it turned out, she was glad for the opportunity for some physical activity. Scarcely looking a full generation older than Dabney in her tee shirt, shorts and tennis shoes, she had been hopping the prescribed combinations with Dabney for perhaps a quarter of an hour when a small, honey-colored Mercedes pulled up.

Yolande Carr got out carrying a leather portfolio and a huge bouquet of azaleas in her arms. Not recognizing Annie, the dark-haired photographer quickly entered the courtyard and climbed the narrow steps to Jake's apartment, her trim yet voluptuous body clad in raw silk slacks and a clinging, short-sleeved sweater. A moment later, Jake's door opened and then closed behind her.

There goes the reason he won't make love to me again, she thought with unhappy certainty. Probably

I'm boring and inexperienced compared with the luscious Miss Carr.

That night there was a familiar face in the audience. To Annie's surprise, she recognized her cousin Zenon Trosclair sitting at a table against the back wall. With him was a heavy-set, older man she didn't know, though he and Zenon bore a striking family resemblance.

Alphonse, she thought with certainty. I don't believe it. He managed to get his father in here to hear me sing. Then an exciting possibility struck her: this dour-looking man with her cousin was also her mother's older brother—someone who would remember her well, if he chose to share those memories.

At the end of the set, she wasn't sure whether or not she'd be welcome at their table. While she debated, the decision was taken out of her hands. Making his way through the crowd, Zenon caught her attention, then presented himself to her with a little bow.

"I see you're wearin' one of those dresses we found in the attic," he said in that deliberate way of his. "It looks mighty nice on you. Papa and I were in town on business this afternoon, and I . . . uh, talked him into catchin' part of your show. He wants to meet you."

Annie smiled, remembering his hesitant kindness. "I'd like that very much," she said.

Alphonse Trosclair got stiffly to his feet as she approached. Even at close range she could detect nothing of Solange in his face.

As Zenon made the introductions, Alphonse offered his hand, then invited her to sit down. "May we buy you a drink, Miss Duprez?" he asked in his heavy voice.

It was an awkward moment. She had no intention of drinking in front of her long-lost and extremely conservative uncle. But she also didn't want to turn down his offer. "Please," she said, "call me Annie. And yes, thank you, I'd love a cola, if that would be all right."

Her tact and restraint brought a faint smile of approval in return. The two of them looked at each other with the wary beginnings of friendliness while Zenon ordered. She could feel Jake staring at her from across the room.

"Now," Alphonse said before his son could add anything to smooth the way, "let me tell you how much you look like your mother. And that you sing as well . . . perhaps better, though of course I'm not a competent judge of such things."

Modestly Annie lowered her eyes. "Thank you," she said. "You're very kind. When . . . would you mind telling me when you heard her sing?"

A ghost of a smile flickered beneath Alphonse's thick gray mustache. "I sneaked into town once when she was performing here, though Papa would have killed me." He chuckled at the look on Zenon's face. "You know something? Though the similarities are striking, there are differences too . . ." He paused as the drinks arrived, and then raised his glass to her in a little salute. "She was a softer person than you, I think," he mused, fixing her with his great brown eyes. "Yes . . . the Cajun fisherman gave you some of his stubbornness."

Annie smiled, pleased that he had acknowledged Ned. "I believe he used to tell me that himself," she said.

Her uncle nodded. "Zenon says your father is dead now, and that you have come to New Orleans to find your mother's past, as well as to establish a singing career of your own." To her surprise, his voice held no note of disapproval. "Zenon is right," he added. "There has been too much estrangement in our family. I'll tell you what I can, though I rarely saw my half sister after she left us."

"Half sister?" Annie asked, fastening on this surprising new piece of information. "I didn't know that."

Alphonse shrugged his massive shoulders. "Solange was the daughter of my father's second wife, who died in childbirth," he explained. "The spoiled one, if you must know the truth, the one who had everything she wished."

He stopped to finish the rest of his drink, then set his glass down on the table and laid some money beside it. "Not that she couldn't be very sweet," he added as if he regretted his frankness. "Sweet like an angel; and just as innocent. As I said, I'll be glad to tell you whatever you like. But not now, in these surroundings. Zenon, your cousin Addie and I are hoping you'll be able to join us for Sunday dinner at Carteret. If you're agreeable, Zenon will pick you up with the car."

Annie considered rapidly. Fortunately, Sunday was a free day from the club and she had both Sunday and Monday off from the restaurant, thanks to her flexible schedule there. Unfortunately, Sunday was also the day that Jake's Aunt Bethia had invited her to attend a birthday celebration.

Well, I won't be expected to put in an appearance at the Jacobsens' *now,* she thought. Jake certainly isn't going to be my escort.

"I'd be delighted, Uncle Alphonse," she replied.

"Good." He gave his leonine head a satisfied shake. For the first time since she'd joined them at their table, Zenon spoke again. "I'll pick you up at about nine, if that's not too early," he said, taking a tiny notebook and pencil out of his pocket to copy the address she gave him.

After they'd left, it still wasn't time for her to go onstage again. Wanting to be alone with her thoughts, she slipped out the back door of the club into the courtyard and stepped back into the shadow of a large banana plant to observe the softly lit fountain.

"You've been avoiding me, you know," said a deep, familiar voice beside her.

It was Jake, of course. Summoning her poise, she turned to face him. "Not quite accurate," she said. "I've been rather busy lately, and so have you."

His cigarette was a brief firefly glow in the dark. "I see you've made some new friends. Who are your gentlemen admirers?"

Annie pushed down the urge to smile. "Not that it's any of your business," she said, "but they happen to be relatives . . . my cousin and my uncle from Vacherie, to be exact. They've invited me out to the plantation for dinner on Sunday."

Her strong satisfaction in being able to make that casual announcement surprised her. Apparently, even this limited contact with her mother's family meant more to her than she had guessed.

Meanwhile, Jake was frowning. "I hope you had the presence of mind to tell them no," he said. "You have a previous engagement."

"I'm not quite sure what you're talking about," she hedged.

"Yes, you are. The birthday dinner at my aunt and uncle's house. Surely you remember it."

"As a matter of fact, I do remember its being

discussed. But as far as I knew, it was never a firm plan. And under the circumstances . . ."

Jake made a little gesture of impatience. "Just what *are* the circumstances, Annie?"

He was being obdurate and he knew it. "You're quite well aware how things stand between us, Jake St. Arnold," she said.

An electric silence rested between them as he blew out a little cloud of smoke. "So you're going, then . . . to Vacherie," he said, making a statement of it.

"Yes," she answered, leaving him no room for argument. "That's exactly what I intend to do."

On Sunday morning, one week to the day after her awkward breakfast *en déshabillé* with Jake, her cousin Zenon arrived to collect her at Sally's apartment. He looked extremely out of place in its bizarre, offbeat setting.

Yet as they made the long trip out to Vacherie, she came once again to see him as a kind and essentially self-directed person, for all his incessant tact and deference to his father.

"Addie's nervous about meeting you," he admitted as they turned off the Mississippi River Bridge and onto the West Bank Expressway. "She's heard a bit too much in the past few days about Solange and how beautiful she was, how much you look like her. Addie's . . . not beautiful. It might be best if you were . . . uh, as unassuming as possible with her. In my opinion, that would be the very best way to win her friendship."

As they drove, he spoke with growing frankness, reminding her of his father's youthful jealousy of Solange. He advised her to go easy with her questions, to be aware of the way jealousy might still color his recollections.

By the time they were pulling into Carteret's long gravel drive opposite the levee, Annie felt as if she had an ally of long standing. But maybe she didn't really need one now. Ascending the broad, steep front steps of the classic Creole farmhouse, Annie remembered her fears at her earlier visit. But today she was arriving as an invited guest, almost as a member of the family.

The spinster Adelaide Trosclair, a pale, feminine version of Zenon, greeted Annie with shy reservation and disappeared almost immediately into the kitchen with her helping woman, Sarah. Together with Zenon, Alphonse took her on a tour of the grounds, showed her the small family plot with its raised vaults, one of which held her mother's remains.

Then they were at the table in the traditionally furnished dining room, with Annie exclaiming over the baked oysters, smothered chicken and bean croquettes until her cousin Addie flushed with praise. But though the conversation became progressively more relaxed, Annie could see that Alphonse was clearly the head of this household, and that table talk followed in the direction he set.

He seemed more than willing to discuss Solange's childhood, telling funny stories about the way she had chased the ducks his father had kept; how she had constantly dressed up in her deceased mother's finery, which she'd dragged down from the attic, to sit at the piano in the parlor and sing for hours. "Herve, my father, wanted her to marry a planter like himself," Alphonse said, touching as closely as he would that day on the years Annie most wanted to learn about. "Such a marriage was on the verge of being arranged when she ran off with young Duprez. Ideas are different today. Maybe now your grandfather could have learned to understand."

As Annie rode back into town with Zenon late that afternoon, she reflected that she'd been wise to heed her cousin's advice and proceed slowly. Addie's farewell had been noticeably warmer than her greeting, and Alphonse appeared to view her as a considered, well-bred young lady despite her Cajun heritage and choice of profession. Briefly, there had been a chance after dinner to sit in the very parlor where Solange had played her dress-up games, and go through the family album.

If she was patient, she might learn more from the Trosclairs in time. Whatever the outcome, it seemed as if the rift in the family had begun to heal.

Zenon dropped her off at the entrance to her apartment courtyard a little after five p.m. Sally was just going out. "There was a phone message for you," her friend called hurriedly. "From a Mrs. Jacobsen. She said if you got back in time, to come on out to the party anyway, and not worry if you couldn't make it for supper."

With Sally gone, Annie wasted the better part of an hour reconsidering the invitation, changing her mind, and then changing it back again. Finally, she gave up in disgust and took her silver gray dress and jacket out of the closet. You know you want to see how Jake's family lives, she acknowledged. You're so curious, you can't stay away. Just don't let yourself have any fantasies of getting involved with him again.

Saving her money for a return taxi after dark, Annie took the inexpensive St. Charles Avenue streetcar, distracting herself with its noisy ramble through a tiny portion of the downtown, the run-down section around Lee Circle, and finally past the gracious old mansions of the Garden District.

As she drew nearer her destination, Annie couldn't stop her thoughts from returning to Jake, and she damned herself for being far too interested in him still. Try to remember, she told herself sharply. You'll be Bethia and John Jacobsen's guest, not his.

The Jacobsen residence, recessed into its parklike setting one block off the streetcar line, was a graceful Italianate structure of white-painted wood with black shutters and ironwork. Fearing she had made the wrong decision to come, Annie mounted the steps to the glittering beveled-glass door and rang the bell.

A maid answered taking her straight to Bethia Jacobsen as soon as she mentioned her name. Supper was obviously over. They found Bethia circulating among her guests in the home's double parlor, a wonder of fourteen-foot ceilings, soft old oriental rugs, and petticoat mirrors beneath the sideboards.

"I'm so glad you could make it after all," Jake's aunt welcomed her. "We're having our after-dinner coffee and cordials. Won't you join us? There are some people I'd like you to meet."

After renewing her acquaintance with Bethia's husband, John, Annie was introduced to more of the other guests than she could possibly remember. As for Jake, she noted in puzzlement that he was nowhere to be seen.

"Almost time to open John's present," a woman friend called gaily to her hostess in passing. "Got your final guess ready and sealed in the envelope?"

Bethia laughed and nodded, then explained to Annie in a low tone that her husband's birthday gifts to her had become more outrageously extravagant and original each year of their marriage. "They've become the highlight of my annual party," she said. "It's getting so people don't want to miss them."

"Then why isn't Jake here?" Annie queried, hating herself for being so obvious. "Didn't he come to the party?"

Bethia gave her an odd look. "I thought you'd never ask. Come with me into the kitchen a moment, will you, while I check on something?"

Mystified, Annie followed her into the cream-tiled kitchen where Bethia attended to a minor detail, then out onto the deserted rear porch, which overlooked the gardens.

"Jake had dinner with us, and I believe he's out in the rose garden now having a solitary smoke," Bethia said. "This is a hard time for him, you know . . . it's a year to the day tomorrow since Jamie was killed."

Annie frowned, a little nameless emotion clutching at her heart. "Who was Jamie?" she asked.

Jake's aunt shook her head, then glanced out at the shadowy garden beyond the balustrade. "I supose I can tell you," she said. "Jamie was Jake's eight-year-old son. He died in an automobile crash along with his mother, in Houston."

Annie's rush of sympathy for Jake was instanteous. "I didn't know. Jake's wife . . ."

Bethia sighed. "Jake and Laurelle were never married . . . not that Jake wasn't willing to marry her, especially after the boy was on the way. But she wouldn't have that . . . took Jamie off to Texas right after he was born when she got a better job offer there. She let Jake have his son in the summers, though. Jamie used to love it here . . . coming out to visit us, playing with Dabney Washington, just hanging out with his dad."

"And . . . and Jake?" Annie whispered.

"He loved that boy more than life. It nearly killed him when he died."

Hot tears threatened to spill down Annie's cheeks. What did it matter if Jake didn't want to want her, if he preferred Yolande Carr to her? In the face of her reaction to what Bethia Jacobsen had revealed, there was no denying it: she loved him with all her heart.

"Would you mind very much if I went out and looked for him, Mrs. Jacobsen?" she asked in a small voice.

Bethia gave her a little hug. "I wouldn't mind in the least, my dear. In fact, that's what I was hoping you would do."

Not sure what she would say to him, Annie walked down the back steps of the Jacobsen mansion and crossed the already dewy lawn in the dark, with only the lantern light from the porch to guide her. She located Jake by the glow of his cigarette. "Hello," she said, stepping into the little rose-covered gazebo and coming up beside him.

Obviously, he'd been aware of her approach. "I thought you weren't coming," he said dryly, the words slightly off-key, so that they had an unnatural ring.

"I changed my mind."

Nothing more was said for a moment as they stood little more than an arm's length apart. Then, "I'm so sorry about your son," she said. "Your aunt told me."

"My God. I can't think why." He turned his back to her and ground out his cigarette.

Behind him, she was a silent presence, waiting.

"Jamie was such a special little boy," he said at last, the words tumbling out in a voice like no other she'd heard from him. "Intelligent. Worldly. In a restaurant he would order prawns instead of the usual kid's hamburger, put the waitress at ease if he asked for lime soda and she brought him a Coke.

"He liked art . . . knew all the old jazz music already, too. Played around a little on the drums. I had him in the summers. I saw to that."

Desperately she wanted to reach out and touch the man she loved, but wasn't sure it would be all right to do it. "Bethia told me," she interjected softly instead.

He glanced at her over his shoulder. "Did she tell you about Laurelle . . . that we weren't ever husband and wife?"

Annie nodded wordlessly.

"I loved her too," he said, looking away again. "Very much. She used to say I didn't, not in the way she needed. That if I did, I'd have wanted her to be free. But that was a long time ago. I got over it. You never get over your own child, though, never stop loving him. Jamie was like a piece of my soul . . ."

His strong, deep voice broke a little on the words.

"Jake," she said, not weighing her actions now as she slid one hand up the broad expanse of his back, so hard under the grainy softness of his raw silk jacket.

"Annie, don't." He passed one hand over his eyes. "Not unless you want to see me cry."

"In God's name, how could you help but do that, sweetheart?" The next moment, her arms were around him and he had turned to face her, to lay his cheek against her hair. She could feel the hot, bitter wetness of his tears.

"I loved him so damn much, you know," he choked. "The frowning, grown-up look he had when he considered something . . . my blue eyes beneath his little-boy lashes . . . just the shape of him that let you guess what kind of man he'd make someday. I can't even tell you how dear he was, how beautifully made . . ."

With a sob, he broke off all speech. Silently shaking, he clung to her as if to a life raft, holding her so tightly she thought her ribs would break. Mutely she pressed herself against him, not knowing how to comfort him but longing to absorb whatever she could of his pain.

After a few moments, he quieted. "I told you I'd make a fool of myself," he said, in better control now though still his voice shook with emotion.

"You haven't done that." Annie reached up to smooth a lock of dark hair from his forehead. "I know I can't comfort you the way Yolande could," she said. "But if it helps to hang on to me, I'm here for as long as you want."

"*Yolande?*" Jake's tone changed to one of incredulity as he drew his dark brows together. "So *that's* what you think . . . I don't suppose I've given you any reason to believe it, Annie, but knowing you . . . making love to you . . . are the best things that have happened to me since Jamie died."

8

Annie looked up at Jake in amazement. Can he really mean it? she asked herself. How could I have been so wrong about what he feels?

As if he sensed her uncertainty, he cupped her chin in his hands, looking deep into her wide gray eyes. "Say you'll let me have you again," he said softly. "Even if I've behaved like a fool."

She felt no real hesitation; immediately, she wanted to tell him yes, straight from the heart. But still she couldn't help wondering why he'd retreated from intimacy only a week before. Was he wary because of what happened between him and Jamie's mother so long ago? Or was there another reason, one she couldn't begin to guess?

"Are you certain that's what you want?" she asked. "Even if you've ravished me, I'm still the decent type."

"And you think I wasn't ravished, my sweet angel, just by making love to you?"

With a fierce little swoop of his dark head, he lowered his mouth to hers. At once she knew the truth: the pain she'd felt during the week of their separation had been no greater than his. This man, whom she'd been trying so hard to forget, had been aching for her touch. Whatever his reasons for behaving the way he had, they hadn't stemmed from any lack of desire.

Something in her soared at the realization. "Jake," she whispered when at last she could speak, "don't you know how much I want you?"

"Maybe I can guess. I've been wanting you the same way, you know, even in my dreams." Unexpectedly, the little lines at the corners of his mouth curved in a wry, fleeting smile. "Do you suppose we could get away from here . . . go somewhere I could mope around if I needed to, feel like hell until this thing passes?"

It was a compliment to her that he would want her with him. And unhesitatingly she knew where they should go. Always, when her heart had ached over childhood insults and tragedies, Ned had brought her out to the swamp, taught her to lose herself in its beauty, to partake of its healing communion.

"I know the perfect spot," she said, silently thanking her father for having been the kind of man he was. "It's a place of water and cypress trees and sky. But it's quite a distance from here . . . an hour and a half's drive at least. And we couldn't take out the boat until morning."

Jake didn't hesitate. "Run in the house and get your things," he told her. "My car's out back. I'll pick you up in five minutes, by the street."

They stopped first at his place and then at Sally's, just

long enough to snatch up a change of clothes. Then
they were driving over the bridge, heading south and
west toward the house where she'd grown up and
dreamed of loving a man like him. Nestled in the curve
of his arm, she wondered how that place would seem
now, filled with his presence.

Now that they were together, her head was full of
tender thoughts and imaginings. But it had been a long,
emotion-filled day. Twenty minutes past Gretna, she
was fast asleep.

He woke her on the outskirts of Houma. It had
started to rain, a gentle spring shower that was like a
blessing. Sleepily, she asked to pull in beside a conve-
nience store so she could pick up some supplies. Then
they were driving through the quiet streets to the far
side of town, pulling in beside Bayou Black and Ned's
shingled cottage. Jake halted his Corvette where Ned
had always parked his pickup.

The reality that it would never be standing there
again hit her with force, and she paused a moment,
fighting back tears.

"You know what it is to lose someone too, don't you,
angel?" Jake asked softly.

The look in his eyes told her she needn't answer
him in words. Giving her a little squeeze, he picked up
the grocery sacks and then followed her to the door.
Annie unlocked it and held it open, standing aside
to let him pass. Depositing the groceries on the
counter, he looked around at neat rag rugs scattered
over worn linoleum, the rounded, old-fashioned refrigerator, a drainboard that was skirted to hide the
pipes.

By now the rain was beating a steady tattoo on the

roof, while they were snug inside the little cottage with each other.

"Come here, Annie," he said.

Unhesitatingly, she went into his arms. For a moment, he simply held her, as if he were grateful to have her as his lifeline when memories of Jamie crowded close. Then, "Why don't I break a few of those eggs into a frying pan?" he asked in a casual tone. "I can't have you doing without supper on my account."

"Thanks," she answered softly, "but I'm not hungry."

"Okay, then. Let's go to bed."

Though he'd hinted they wouldn't make love that night, she didn't offer him his own room. "In here," she said, leading him to her small bedroom. The double bed, an ancient mattress atop squeaky, open springs, was about half the size of the huge four-poster in his apartment.

"Got a shower?" he inquired, placing a kiss on the tip of her nose and stripping off his things without ceremony.

Annie nodded, pointing in the proper direction. She found herself staring at his splendid physique—all compact muscle, with dark hair covering his chest and arms and legs in a way that profoundly attracted her. His son would have looked like him someday, she thought with a sudden twinge, able to understand a little of his sorrow.

At the moment, he seemed relaxed and even mildly happy. Yet she knew from her experience with her father how closed a man could be when he was hurt. And she realized he wouldn't want to make it a habit to cry. His openness in Bethia's garden would not be repeated very soon, she thought. And it was going to be difficult sleeping with him and not having him the way she wanted.

As Annie came out of the shower, she saw that he was already under the covers, the hair about his ears still a little damp from bathing. Stretched out full length on the side where she usually slept, he smoked and watched her as she dried off and then reached for a nightgown.

"You don't need that, Annie," he said abruptly, putting out his cigarette and drawing back the covers. "If we're going to be sleeping together, we don't want modesty between us."

That night, although he didn't make love to her before they slept, a feeling very much like love seemed to bind them together. In that intimate embrace, the splendor and warmth of him seemed to suffuse her very soul, making her feel safe and cherished, a part of everything he was.

I love you so much, Jake, she told him silently as she drifted off to sleep in his arms. But I'm afraid that what we now share can't last. You won't risk losing someone again. And I . . . I daren't pay the price. I'd never want to make my mother's mistakes with you. But for now . . . few lovers are lucky enough to experience what I have here with you tonight.

Morning came, and with it cooler, sunnier weather. For a moment Annie was startled, ready to panic when she realized he was gone from her bed again. But then he walked in naked from the bathroom to confess that he had borrowed her toothbrush, and she knew everything was all right.

It struck her that she must appear a little silly, caught

kneeling on the bed with the covers clutched around her. "You look like some wood nymph, startled to awareness by a mortal's gaze," he observed, that errant blue glint coming alive in his eyes again. "Why not drop the sheet and let me appreciate you?"

Slowly, she did as he asked. She could feel her breasts firm and swell as he looked at them, her rosy nipples harden with desire.

"How absolutely lovely you are," he murmured, climbing on the bed opposite her so that they were kneeling face-to-face.

It wasn't any secret in this intimate juxtaposition that his need was as great as hers. Tangling his fingers in her halo of blond hair, he raised her mouth to his and invaded it languidly, as if he meant to take possession of it forever.

Removed as they were from the demands of their day-to-day existence, they could afford to indulge a sense of timelessness. Yet already there were hints in the way they caressed each other that such leisure wouldn't last.

Lost in what was happening between them, Annie couldn't know how right their bodies looked together, how primal and beautiful they were in motion. At that moment, she could only feel—sharp stabs of longing exquisitely at odds with his tenderness as he touched her breasts; a fire that seemed to flow through her veins as he grasped her buttocks to pull her up against him.

"I've been out of my mind with wanting you," she confessed, running her hands over the hard muscles of his back and shoulders. "Night and day, I've thought of nothing but having you again."

"You'll have me, baby, never fear." His voice was rough with an urgency that was rapidly moving out of bounds. Drawing her down beside him against the pillows, he parted her legs with one muscular, aggressive thigh.

"Jake," she gasped, opening to receive him.

"We'll have time later to play, Annie. Right now, I can't wait. I need you."

There would be no sweet, slow initiation. But Annie didn't care about that at all. She, too, needed him, and his possession of her, so powerful and strong, nearly set her off in a cascade of rapture.

But though he edged her back from the brink with a mastery he himself had nearly lost, she didn't have long to wait. In what seemed only moments, they were holding tightly to each other as they shuddered out of control, their path to glory marked by little cries and kisses and whispers.

Finally they quieted. Unwilling to draw apart, they drifted down from the heights together—still one person in spirit, Annie thought, though the peak of physical unity had passed. For her part, she was still glowing like an ember in his arms.

"My God, but I love you," Jake whispered, gently smoothing back a damp tendril of hair from her forehead and kissing her mouth.

"I love you too." The words seemed to come from some spontaneous and guileless place deep within herself. At the moment, she wasn't thinking of the future at all.

When they awoke again, it was after ten o'clock. While Jake prepared their breakfast of scrambled eggs, toast and *café au lait,* she went outside and readied the boat. Soon he was standing next to her at the wheel, dressed in one of her father's old windbreakers, as she maneuvered them under the bridge and through the gate into Miners' Canal, an old logging channel that led directly to the swamp.

"You're quite a cook," she told him, narrowing her eyes a little against the brilliant sunlight. "I stuffed myself like one of thse old gators out in the swamp."

Crinkles of amusement appeared at the corners of his mouth, and though she couldn't see past his dark glasses, she could imagine the lively humor in his eyes.

"They say love makes you fierce," he replied.

Annie gave a contented little shrug. "I don't know about that. But it certainly does make me hungry."

He put one arm around her. "Where are we going?" he asked, forced to shout a little now that she had increased their speed and the rush of wind threatened to swallow up their voices.

She smiled, happy with the scent of air and the damp feel of the spray against her face, his presence beside her. "To some secret and lovely places. A wild iris garden that would put Xochimilco to shame. My father's old trapping camp, and the water meadows where nutria and muskrats feed. Lake Hatch, where Ned knew all the alligators by name."

"Ned?" he asked.

"My father. That's what I used to call him."

They couldn't have asked for a better day. Ahead, the soothing, endless vista of water and sky awaited. The breeze was picking up and birds were singing in the willows that lined the banks of the waterway. To stern, their wake churned up the water of the channel in shimmering droplets.

Turning first into one connecting waterway and then another, Annie guided them ever deeper into the trackless southern Louisiana wilderness of floating marsh and distant oil rigs, under vast, brooding cypresses and tupelo gums, past the lonely little islands of higher ground.

Compared with New Orleans, it was a different world. Here, blackberries grew wild and turtles swam, sunlight dipped in lazy diamonds on the water. Where the earth was solid enough to support them, swamp maples hung with muscadine vines reddened in first leaf, while the gray, moss-bearded cypresses, their grotesque knees protruding from the water, still languished in winter nakedness.

"What bird was that?" Jake asked, picking up the binoculars from the dash beside her and raising them to follow the direction of its flight.

Annie glanced after it briefly. "A yellow-crowned night heron, I think. You can tell by the dark head and the high-pitched call. We have maybe a million kinds of birds out here. For many of them this is the mating season."

"But not all?"

She shook her head. "See that clump of twigs and dried grass in the dead cypress? That's a bald eagle's nest. They leave in May, come back by September, lay their eggs before Christmas. And then there are the ducks . . ."

Slowing the boat a little, she instructed Jake to dip his hand in the greenish slime that covered the surface of a shallow pool just outside the channel.

"That's duckweed," she said, as he brought up a handful of tiny emerald-colored floating plants glistening with water droplets. "One of the world's smallest flowering botanical wonders. Ducks consider it a rare delicacy. They descend on it as voraciously as I ate your delicious breakfast this morning."

The duckweed carpet churned up like confetti in their wake as they moved on. Jake was giving her a thoughtful look.

"You really know the swamp, don't you, Annie?" he said.

She shrugged. "I grew up with it, I guess. But it was my father's whole life."

"Yet not yours? I wonder if you'll be happy in the long run, exchanging all this for a city existence, your nocturnal singing career."

"I'll be happy. It'll be enough to come back to the swamp now and then, when I need its peace."

Slowing the boat even more, Annie eased them into a winding, moss-draped opening in the trees. Then she turned off the engine altogether so that they drifted inside what might have been the vestibule of a cypress cathedral, all dappled by sunlight and shadow.

"Look ahead of you, darling," she whispered. "This is one of those iris gardens I told you about."

Some thirty feet beyond them, in a navelike clearing that was too shallow for a boat, the exotic blue and purple flowers were massed in delicate profusion atop tall, rapierlike stems.

"They're incredibly beautiful," Jake breathed, matching her hushed tones, and lacing his fingers through hers. "I know that's trite to say. But it's what I feel. You were right to bring me here today, sweetheart. It's a healing kind of place."

She didn't reply, but only leaned her head against his shoulder. They stood there in silence for several minutes behind the wheel of her father's boat, gazing in awe at nature's secret chapel while water lapped gently against the hull. Quietly echoing, the soft chorus of swamp sounds filtered into their consciousness.

"Let met tell you a bit more about Laurelle," he said finally, squeezing her hand and leaning back against the cracked and peeling leather seat. "I was young, twenty-seven or twenty-eight, when we had our affair. She was a good person, in her way . . . decent, as you've probably guessed. I thought I wanted to marry her, tried to insist when I learned she was carrying my child."

He fell silent, tapping out a cigarette and lighting it as he cupped his hands about the flame.

"She refused," he continued after a moment. "She was a stockbroker, and her career meant everything. Right after Jamie was born, she had an offer in Houston for nearly twice the money she was making. My career and my life were here. So she took my son off to Texas with her."

There was a small silence as Jake rested his gaze on the wild beauty of the irises, as if seeking balm for a long-standing hurt. "I wouldn't let that happen again if I had it to do over," he added roughly. "I'd fight, try to get Jamie's custody myself. But we had some good times together anyway. I saw him as much as I could . . ."

His pain wasn't as sharp and raw today, though she knew instinctively that the current of it still ran deep. "Bethia told me how happy the two of you were together," she said.

"Yeah. We were," he answered, then fell silent.

He wasn't going to say anything more for the moment. Biting her lip, Annie started up the boat again, backed out into the channel.

Maybe I love Jake, she told herself, but I'm the wrong person to help him get over Jamie's death. If he's to marry someday and father another child to fill the empty place in his heart, he needs a woman he can count on.

Pensive and a little withdrawn, she let the engine idle as they approached Ned's old trapping shack. Set on a tiny patch of higher ground, it was little more than a makeshift lean-to of scrap lumber and tin, barely offering protection from the elements.

"My father leased the fishing and trapping rights to this place for years," she told Jake. "The lease is due for renewal again this month. I suppose someone else will be using it now."

He gave her a sympathetic look. "What was he like?" he asked, mistaking the cause of her faint sadness.

"Ned?" She tried to picture her father's face. "Just a quiet, old-fashioned man of simple tastes . . . one who, when he loved, loved for a lifetime."

"That's how it should be." Jake paused. "Don't get me wrong . . . I'm not thinking of Laurelle. In some ways it made sense for her to leave me. The kind of love we had together wasn't meant to last."

Determined to lighten her mood for his sake, Annie shrugged off her feelings of melancholy as best she could. "I'm sure you're right," she jibed affectionately. "You haven't exactly been pining away, have you, with Yolande Carr waiting in the wings?"

Jake grinned, his thoughts distracted from the past. "Can it be that you're jealous, angel?" he asked. "I haven't given you cause."

"Is that so? I seem to remember the lady in question trudging up to your apartment less than a week ago, with a bouquet of azaleas in her arms."

His grin broadened. "I was certain you'd seen her," he replied. "I was watching from the window when she arrived. But it wasn't what you suppose. She stopped by with some photographs of a building project we just completed out at Tulane. Oh, I don't deny she brought me flowers. Or that she's interested in me. But I haven't even thought about the beauteous Miss Carr in some time, certainly not since I met you."

Annie couldn't suppress her joy at his words. "I'm delighted to hear it," she told him.

"And I take the greatest pleasure in your delight."

Slipping one hand inside her jacket, he unbuttoned several buttons on her blouse, loosened the front closure on her bra.

"So warm and delicious," he said, baring her to his touch. "There can't be any breasts more beautiful than these in all the world. Do you think we might take that old blanket you brought and stretch out here on the property while you still have a right to it? Or would the gators nibble on our toes?"

Though they'd made love only a few hours before, she could feel her body grow heavy again with wanting him. "I think we definitely could risk it," she said.

The sun was much lower in the sky when finally they headed for Lake Hatch, opening the water gate with Ned's key. Just as her father had always done when she was a child, she whistled and called for the alligators by name—Babe and Little Huey and Dumpling and Max —feeding them pieces of raw chicken from the end of a stick for Jake's amusement.

I always want to please him as I have today, she thought, relieved at the way the tension had eased from his shoulders, at the lively look that had returned to his beautiful eyes. Above all, I long to make him happy. Never to hurt. I wish things *could* go on this way forever.

9

Back in the city, Annie and Jake spent nearly all their free moments together. Though officially she still resided at Sally's and paid her share of the rent each week, she spent every night in Jake's big bed, drawing so close to him in both body and spirit that it frightened her to think they could ever be apart. And so she pushed any such thought away. Instead, she wanted only to drift through the bright spring days in a haze of desire and fulfillment, losing herself in his love and in the old songs she sang at the club to ever more enthusiastic crowds.

Throughout it all, she didn't forget her quest to learn about her mother's life. Unfortunately, there were no new leads, and in this one aspect of her life she remained frustrated. Despite diligent checking on Harry's part, they were no closer to finding Marie Arnogne —if she was actually still alive—than they had ever been. Annie was left with only Alphonse Trosclair's recollections of Solange as a spoiled young girl who had dreamed of becoming a singer someday, and Harold Dorsey's memories of a shallow, promiscuous woman.

Added to the mute evidence of the role Solange had played in her father's life, neither reminiscence boded well for her relationship with Jake. If she'd inherited her mother's restlessness and single-minded dedication to a career, as she believed, allowing herself to fall in love with him was nothing more than inviting disaster.

Yet she could no more stop herself than hold back the wind. I'm not getting any job offers from New York, nor any proposals of marriage from Jake, she thought; I don't have to deal with the issue yet. I love him, and at the moment, I couldn't turn my back on him if I tried.

Yet frightening as it was, the prospect of having a permanent relationship with him appealed to her at some deep and elemental level. The possibility that, if she left him someday, some other woman might take her place and bear him a child to replace Jamie was too painful even to think about.

Meanwhile, Jake was spending fewer hours at the club. His every free moment went into Stephen Morel's St. Petersburg project, whether in his architectural office or the workroom he had set up in his apartment. Interested in everything that was important to the man she loved, Annie hung about whenever he worked at home, watching the final plans for the multimillion-dollar structure take shape.

Florida Centre was to be an immense, energy-efficient office, banking and commercial complex situated around a planted atrium, overlooking the Tampa Bay waterfront.

"Morel told me he wanted a world-class building,"

Jake told her with satisfaction over his littered drawing table one evening. "I think I've given it to him here."

The following Friday, Stephen Morel himself arrived in New Orleans to pass judgment. At Jake's insistence, Annie begged time off from her job at the oyster bar to be present for the presentation at his office. "I want you to be part of everything in my life," he told her.

Though initially she felt out of place sitting by silently in the impressive conference room, she soon put any awkwardness aside as she became absorbed in the presentation. She was fascinated by Jake's competence and flair, his commitment to excellence.

Morel—plainly a sophisticated and exacting man, as well as a person of considerable wealth and connection —wasn't bothering to hide his approval and esteem. "You've done a damn fine job with the project, St. Arnold," he commented finally when Jake had concluded his presentation. "It's everything I bargained for and more. Let's break out the champagne."

To Annie's surprise, it was a literal suggestion, doubtless based on the developer's past experience with the firm. On cue, John Jacobsen picked up the conference room phone, and a minute later a secretary was bringing in a magnum of the bubbly stuff along with four chilled glasses. Jake did the honors, popping the cork with the proper Gallic élan.

"Allow me to propose a toast," Morel suggested smoothly.

With a nod and his quick, confident smile, Jake deferred.

"To Florida Centre . . . may it enhance our reputations and make us all a great deal of money," Morel proposed, raising his glass. "And to Miss Annie Duprez, who has graciously shown her interest in our project, and who will entertain us so richly tonight with her beautiful voice."

Turning his forthright hazel gaze on her with undisguised admiration, he made no secret of his attraction to her, despite the fact that Jake was not only his business associate but his friend. Out of the corner of her eye, she could see John Jacobsen raising an eyebrow, feel Jake's quiet appraisal of the situation.

"I . . . hardly know what to say, Mr. Morel," Annie replied, throwing Jake a glance. "I know very little about architecture, but still I'd like to add my congratulations to yours, and compliment Jake on an extraordinary job."

Jake's uncle threw her a grateful look. "As the senior partner in this firm, I heartily second the motion," he said.

They drank, Morel eyeing Annie over the rim of his glass as if to acknowledge her involvement with Jake—but with the proviso that he might consider challenging it. She could feel his interest as a tangible thing, and it continued unabated all through the celebration supper out at the Jacobsen mansion.

I hope it goes no further than this, Annie thought, as he watched her across the dinner table with the look of a man who is used to getting what he wants.

"My client's quite taken with you," Jake noted with a wicked smile as he settled her in the Corvette when it was time for the two of them to leave for the club. "I hope the feeling isn't mutual."

Deliberately, she laid one hand on his hard-muscled thigh as he got in behind the wheel. "I doubt very much if you're worried about that, Jake St. Arnold," she said.

His smile broadened. They were still parked in the Jacobsens' driveway, and he was showing no inclination to depart. "You're right, I'm not," he acknowledged. "There are some very powerful arguments to be made in my favor."

Annie gave him an innocent look, excited though she was by his masculine assurance. "Care to be more specific?" she asked.

"In words? Or shall I simply demonstrate?" Leaning over to feather little kisses at the corners of her mouth, he slid one hand up the length of her thigh. "I can do a better job of showing you at home tonight," he added. "For now, do you think my word will be good enough?"

As always, her passion for him flared close to the surface. "Yes, Jake," she breathed, going weak all over with what he could make her feel. "Oh, yes. Darling, you know I don't want anyone but you."

That night at the club, singing with the quintet while Jake played host to Morel, John and Bethia at his table, Annie felt she was performing better than ever before. By now, she had become accustomed to the musicians and they to her, so that they played off of each other naturally and gracefully.

Beyond the glare of the lights, the audience that had once looked to her like a sea of impersonal faces now seemed a gathering of friends. Even the nervousness she still experienced as she walked up to the microphone was colored with exhilaration. She retained just enough stage fright and uncertainty to do her best.

But the conviction of mastery she had that night was more than the sum of those parts, she knew. In some way that she couldn't completely define, it was part of her love for Jake, and her fulfillment in giving him everything she was.

Knowing that another man admired her and envied

him their intimacy only enhanced her pride in that gift of self. The experience of loving him so completely, when before she'd despaired of any heart to give, inevitably flowed out in the music.

Annie followed a fast-paced, pull-out-the-stops number with a romantic ballad, and she sang it straight to Jake. Shamelessly she made love to him with her voice, her eyes, her every gesture.

That he adored every moment of her unabashed tribute, she had little doubt. His blue eyes gleaming at her, the little lines she loved quirking beside his mouth, he let his cigarette burn down to ashes in the square glass tray at his elbow as he gave her his undivided attention. When she concluded the set to a storm of applause and returned to his table, he got to his feet and took her into his arms.

"Jazz angel," he whispered, kissing her. "I love you so much."

Stephen Morel and John Jacobsen had arisen courteously, while Bethia beamed her approval. Unwilling to settle for a handshake as Jake's uncle had, Morel kissed her lightly on the cheek and then sat down again with an air of amicable patience.

"There's a proposition I'd like to discuss with you, Annie," he remarked a few minutes later while Jake and his relatives were occupied with someone who had stopped by their table.

When she didn't reply immediately, the wealthy developer continued as if she'd spoken. "My firm and several others in St. Petersburg are organizing our annual picnic and open-air concert for the public in Straub Park, along the waterfront," he said.

"Despite the fact that the symphony will play, it's essentially a pops event. This year, we're featuring music of the forties, though we'll have our traditional *1812* Overture as the finale, complete with cannon and fireworks.

"It's beautiful now in Florida. I'd be honored if you'd consider taking time out here to perform as a soloist for us. All expenses would be paid, of course, and a suite in my condominium would be put at your disposal. I'm sure I don't have to tell you . . . you'd be paid handsomely as well."

Annie had heard him out in silence. Now she slowly shook her head. "Thank you, but no," she said without hesitation. "I'm very flattered that you'd want me. Jake has told me your credentials as a jazz buff are the finest. But I'm under contract here. . . . And besides, I really don't want to leave at the moment."

Morel shrugged, smiled his winning, patient smile. "Naturally I'm not blind to the situation between you and St. Arnold," he said. "Just the same . . . I hope you'll think it over, Annie. We have a week or so yet before we need to have somebody under contract. It would be a good credit for you to have. And I have some excellent contacts who might be useful in advancing your career."

The following day, Jake and Annie took Oscar Washington to the hospital. During the night, his gall bladder had given him trouble again—and this time surgery seemed a possibility. Annie feared seriously for his welfare.

But when Annie returned with Jake to the hospital that afternoon, Oscar's nausea was under control, and the pain in his abdomen had lessened. Just the same, he appeared quite uncomfortable with the needle from an intravenous bottle attached to the vein in one bony hand, and the nasal suction apparatus protruding from one nostril.

"What did you come up here for, Annie?" he asked, shaking his gray head disapprovingly against the pillow. "I don' look like no hotshot mentor today."

Annie smiled at his reference to a remark she'd made several days before, when she'd insisted that the elderly piano player was her mentor. "You're always going to be a hotshot to me," she assured him affectionately. "When are you getting out of here, anyway? Is there anything we can do?"

Oscar gave a heartfelt sigh. "Don' guess I'll be out for a while," he said. "If you'd care to do somethin', you could check on Dabney. He ain't stayed alone before."

"I've arranged for Jimmy Darnell to sleep over at your place for a few days," Jake put in, stepping forward. "And I'll keep an eye on Dabney myself. I want you to stop worrying about him and concentrate on getting well. Paradise Lost is just that . . . lost without you."

Two days later, Annie spied Dabney Washington drawing chalk pictures on the sidewalk in midafternoon, at a time when he should have been in school. As casually as she could, she opened a conversation with him.

"That's a pretty good portrait of Michael Jackson you've got there," she said, tilting her head to one side as she viewed his chalk creation. "But I don't suppose you'll ever be a famous artist. Too bad."

Dabney, who doubtless had been expecting a lecture, looked up with curiosity at such a novel approach. "How come, Miss Annie?" he said. "My grandpa says I can be whatever I want to be."

She shrugged. "You can. Or rather, you could . . . if you took the trouble to go to school and get an education."

Hands thrust into the pockets of his jeans, Dabney made a face. "I knew you'd say something about that," he admitted. "I do go, most of the time anyway. But I just *can't*, today. I don't have anybody to bring with me for Career Day in Miss Ettington's class."

Further questioning revealed that he and his classmates took turns inviting members of their families to talk to the students about their jobs. Today was Dabney's turn, and he had invited Oscar. Now his grandfather was sick in the hospital.

"I'll just tell Miss Ettington I didn't feel good," he explained. "I don't have any other family . . . only him."

"Well . . . you've got friends," rejoined Annie slowly, giving him a quizzical look.

"Like Mister Jake?"

"Yes. And . . .?"

"Like you?"

She nodded.

"You mean *you'd* come?" Sudden enthusiasm glowed in Dabney's lively brown eyes. "You'd really talk to the class?"

"Since you ask, I'd be delighted," Annie said.

Dabney's school was situated only a short distance from the club. The old-fashioned two-story building of stucco painted a dull Chinese red was set back from the street behind a dirt play yard, in the shade of several huge magnolias. As a teacher herself, Annie noted with interest the many signs of a caring and creative staff. A garden area had been set aside for the school's inner-city students, with plots marked off by classroom number. The little project was overrun with a cheerful mixture of vegetables and flowers: marigolds and melons, pansies and green onions, carrots and snap beans and daisies. Hand-painted slogans proclaimed "With Love We Grow" and "Children Are Our Most Valuable Resource."

Dabney's classroom lived up to Annie's expectations. After a few words of introduction by Miss Ettington, she was comfortably seated on the edge of the teacher's desk, relating to thirty wide-eyed youngsters what it was like to be a singer in a cabaret. Dabney, in a front-row seat, beamed with pride.

At the end of her talk, Annie answered questions. Finally Miss Ettington, a freckled redhead about Annie's age, encouraged a round of applause from her students. Startled, Annie turned toward the doorway, where she heard clapping louder than any nine-year-old could produce.

To her astonishment, Jake was lounging there, with a smile on his face that was full of approbation. Just then, the bell rang. "I belong to Dabney too," he told the class in an amused tone. "I've come to collect him and his attractive spokeswoman, if school's over for the day."

"How'd you know where to find us?" Annie asked a few minutes later, as they walked down toward the river to buy Dabney a promised ice cream cone.

"Joe, one of the surrey drivers, saw you go." He laced his fingers through hers while Dabney skipped ahead. "That was a very nice thing you did for the boy," he said warmly, "taking the trouble to go with him to his school."

Annie shrugged, a little embarrassed. "It was nothing," she said.

"Not everybody would do it, though. Seeing you in front of that class makes it possible for me to visualize you as a teacher."

She didn't answer. I've put all that behind me, she thought.

"And it helps me to picture something else," he persisted.

They had halted for a moment at the corner of Royal Street to wait for traffic. "Aren't you going to ask me what that is?" Jake prompted.

How I love him, Annie thought, gazing up into those dark-fringed eyes. The strong, capable feel of his hand in hers made her feel treasured and safe. My world is a better place because of him, she admitted. Just having his company and attention today makes me glad to be alive.

Still, she wasn't sure she wanted to hear what was on his mind.

"I can picture you with a child," he went on, unerringly voicing her unspoken fears. "Loving a child. And not just a helpless little baby, either. A medium-sized, rough-and-tumble kid Dabney's age."

Or Jamie's, she added silently. The two had been friends and playmates. If your son had lived, and you had won his custody the way you wanted, he'd probably have been in Dabney's classroom today. You can't help but be thinking of that.

But even while her heart went out to him at the forthright way he'd spoken, she was beginning to get an uneasy feeling about the direction of his thoughts.

"I've never considered having children of my own," she countered, not liking the way that sounded, but

140

adding irritably to herself that she was speaking the truth.

"I didn't either, before it happened to me," he replied as they started across the street. "But I think that now, if the circumstances were right, I'd plan quite deliberately to create my heir."

Dabney was dancing up and down beside the cart of an ice cream vendor, waiting for them. His chatter about the relative merits of chocolate and praline and rum raisin flavors gave Annie a moment to recover her poise.

Fool that she was, Jake's talk of purposefully fathering a child had made her go weak with longing. Unbidden images of the two of them making love with that object in mind were flashing in her imagination. She could picture herself with his wedding ring on her finger, carrying his baby—imagine his deep love for the small son or daughter who would ease the hurt of Jamie's loss.

"What kind of cone would you like, sweetheart?"

Annie realized that Jake was addressing her with patient amusement, as if he had spoken the words at least once before.

"Oh . . . lemon ice, I think."

She damned herself for letting her voice sound so shaky. I'll be lost if we don't change the subject and soon, she thought. My emotions and my maternal instincts are conspiring to defeat me. But if I give in, even to daydreams of what he's suggesting, I'll have done the most unethical thing I could possibly do. In the final analysis, I'm my mother's daughter, not the angel he believes.

Ice cream cones in hand, the three of them strolled past the artists displaying their works on the iron-grilled fence around Jackson Square. They went in at the gate, admiring the equestrian statue of the hero of New Orleans, still proudly protecting the city from the British after so many years.

A jazz group was playing on the bandstand under the trees, and it had drawn a small crowd. Pigeons were alighting in hopes of catching a few crumbs. On the other side of the park, a steel-drum player had gathered a little knot of listeners of his own. Just then the deep-throated whistle of one of the steamboats that plied the river split the air.

"C'mon, Mister Jake, Miss Annie," Dabney urged, tugging at their hands. "That's the *Robert E. Lee* takin' off. Let's hurry up an' see her."

Jake clasped him on one small-boy shoulder. "You go ahead, Dabney," he said with a smile. "You can run faster than we can. We'll catch up with you."

"Okay!" As quickly as his short legs could carry him, Dabney raced out of the park and across Decatur Street, threading his way through the swish of traffic with all the natural grace of a city-born child. A moment later he was dashing past the fountains by the Café du Monde and up the steps of the famous Moon Walk, a raised promenade atop the levee, which overlooked the river.

Jake slipped one arm about Annie's shoulder. "I just wanted a minute alone with my best girl," he said, tilting her chin with one finger so that she was forced to meet his eyes. "A chance to kiss her, and find out why she's suddenly being so quiet with me."

Not sure how to answer him, Annie simply stood there gazing up at him, a study in mixed emotions.

"Still not talking, hmmm?" He lowered his mouth to

hers to nuzzle it in a series of little kisses that left her defenseless.

"You can't expect me not to take advantage, when you look at me like that," he said finally. "Come to think of it, neither of us has to work tonight. Let's have a look at this steamboat of Dabney's so I can spirit you home and show you just how irresistible you are."

10

Making love in the afternoons, hidden away in Jake's apartment from the bustle of the French Quarter as it awoke to its nocturnal rhythms, had become something of a regular occurrence in Annie's life. When they were both free during that part of the day—she from her job at the oyster bar and he from the demands of his architectural office or running the club—they would go upstairs together by unspoken consent.

Kicking off their shoes and unbuttoning their outer clothing, they intentionally wouldn't touch right away, though they might brush as if by accident against each other's hand, or thigh, or shoulder.

Instead, to prolong the anticipation, they would limit themselves to caressing each other with their eyes. Usually Jake would fix them each a drink, iced tea perhaps, or something stronger if it were past three o'clock or so. She would pad barefoot into the kitchen after him, lean on the island counter topped with a thick slab of rouge Antibes marble, and watch him take the ice and chilled glasses out of the refrigerator.

Sometimes they would begin to play a little there, with Jake teasing her into removing the last of her undergarments while she feigned reluctance, or Annie filching an ice chip and running it unexpectedly over the beautifully formed muscles of his arm and shoulder. Yelping in surprise, he would pin her against the counter exactly the way she wanted.

As they sipped at their drinks, they would begin to kiss—slowly at first, taking delightful and outrageous one-handed liberties with each other. Inevitably their kisses would deepen and grow serious, their caresses become more provocative and forthright. Soon, both hands would be needed. Setting their drinks aside, they would concentrate on the absorbing task of arousal.

If he wanted to be the aggressor that day, Jake might insist on keeping her in the kitchen for a while as he brought her to a series of quivering peaks before sweeping her off to bed in his arms. When it was her turn, and he wished to be passive and adored, she might drop to her knees on the Sarouk runner that lay across the cool tile floor and grant him the same rapturous pleasures.

The end result was always the same: the two of them joined in his big bed under its mosquito-netting canopy, striving in unison to wrest from the gods that most sublime of mortal prizes, the mysterious and soul-nourishing chalice of male-female communion.

Afterward they would lie spent together, pulling up smooth sheets and drifting off to a blissful hour or two of sleep in the safety and contentment of each other's arms. Later, if they were at the club, the looks they'd exchange in that smoky and crowded atmosphere would be full of what the afternoon had held.

You're mine, his blue eyes would remind her, gleaming at her from across the room. *Yes,* her gray ones would respond. *And I love it, being so full of you.*

This afternoon was different. Annie felt the change immediately as Jake unlocked the door and they went inside, shutting it behind them. There was something electric in the air, something serious—a message that shone forth in his eyes but which she was a little afraid to read, just as she'd been reluctant earlier to learn what was on his mind.

He didn't put his thoughts immediately into words. Instead, he settled his hands on her shoulders and looked down at her with a questioning expression.

"Do you know how special you are, Annie?" he asked after a moment. "How important you are in my life?"

Tongue-tied, she couldn't find the right words to answer him. Oh Jake, she pleaded silently. Don't take risks with me. Please, darling . . . just let things go on as they've been . . .

With a little shake of his head, he bent to kiss her hair, her nose, her eyelids, even as his hands moved lower to cover her breasts. "So elusive," he murmured. "Still so separate, as close as we've become. Can you guess how I ache to really *have* you, force you to give your every secret into my keeping?"

Just the way he was touching her, with his thumbs rubbing her nipples through the cotton fabric of her blouse, was making her feel ripe and heavy with longing. Almost by instinct she thrust herself forward,

146

and he caught her sharply up against him, allowing her to feel his need.

I'm ready in seconds for him now, Annie admitted, willfully losing the thread of what he was saying in the hot flowering of her own desire. Maybe I should pull away, walk out of here and out of his life before I cause him any real unhappiness. But when he does these things to me, I can't help myself. I'm a prisoner of what I feel.

With a little groan, as if he'd been temporarily defeated by both her responsiveness and her silence, Jake drew her up the winding stairs to his bed. But she knew he hadn't given up yet. After undressing her, he removed his own tan linen trousers and white shirt and tossed them aside on the floor.

As she stood there with her shoulder-length curtain of blond hair falling across her forehead, Annie watched him with bated breath. Today his eyes held a fierce determination—and more of that incandescent blue fire she loved than she'd ever seen before, even in their most incendiary moments. Things *have* changed between us, she thought, and I'm a little afraid. But I can no more resist him than the tide.

With kisses rapacious and loving against her skin, he lowered her to the bed and covered her with the hard length of his body. "I meant what I said down at the square," he told her as he gently nudged her legs apart. "Don't pretend you didn't understand me. You'd have to be blind, deaf and dumb not to know how I feel about you, or guess the way I catch fire just thinking I could give you a child someday—"

"Jake, please!" The words burst from her in a little rush even as something vulnerable inside her asserted

147

for the first time its feminine craving. "Knowing that's what you want makes me want it too. But I *mustn't* . . . Darling, I'm not ready for that. I might never be."

"Maybe not. I can't help wanting it, all the same."

His mouth on hers, he silenced any reply. As deliberate and forceful as she'd ever known him to be, he set about showing her with his body what she wouldn't accept from him in words, coercing her into imagining what it might be like to open herself to that ultimate surrender.

Completing their loving union, he began to move the way he played his music—establishing an inexorable rhythm, letting emotion flare in a brief hesitation, and then thrusting deeper still until she felt he had all of her, the uttermost reaches of herself. Swept away to heights they'd never before achieved together, she was as shining and helpless as a cymbal, crashing and gleaming at his loving onslaught.

God help me, she thought, only half-coherent seconds before she dissolved in a shuddering storm of ecstasy. But I *want* to have his child, to have him forever.

Reason returned, and with it a certain pensive quietness. Somewhat subdued as he lay propped up against the pillows, Jake smoked and watched the slow revolutions of the ceiling fan without speaking. It's as if he's waiting for an answer, she thought, burying her face in the pillow and stubbornly closing her eyes. As if he believes the assault of his love could have changed my mind.

Yet despite the distance she sensed between them for the first time since they'd returned from the swamp, she was able to fall into a restless sleep. When she awoke, it was much later; the quality of light admitted by the antique wooden shutters had diffused and changed. Jake, sitting comfortably naked in one of the rattan and leather chairs, was just putting down the phone.

Stretching, he got to his feet and held out his hands to her. "Now that Morel has approved the final plans for Florida Centre, and we're about to let bids, I want to celebrate," he said, his blue eyes glinting again with their customary liveliness. "I thought we might blow some of the profits tonight . . . on a real Creole dinner at my favorite restaurant."

Showering together restored some of the closeness they'd lost. Far from being pensive now, Jake seemed to be his most affable and gracious self, as if he had set himself to disarm her. She felt strongly that he'd come to some sort of conclusion and now had a plan in mind, though he wasn't ready to reveal it to her yet.

It was nearly dusk by the time they entered the discreetly tasteful foyer of Arnaud's Restaurant. Jake had called ahead for reservations while she slept. Debonair and darkly handsome in snowy shirt, charcoal gray suit and tie, he was greeted with warmth and deference by the concierge at the desk and by the maître d', who assured M'sieur St. Arnold his table was ready.

"Robert will be your waiter tonight," the maître d' told them, giving the name its French pronunciation as he showed them to a secluded corner table near the etched, frosted front windowpanes. Solicitously, he pulled out Annie's bentwood chair. *"Bon appetit,"* he added. "I trust you will both enjoy your evening."

Looking about her, Annie was glad she'd worn her most elegant street-length dress, a bateau-necked black sheath that fastened with tiny straps at the shoulders.

For Arnaud's was the epitome of elegance. Its clientele was obviously well-to-do and, for the most part, well dressed. Waiters in faultless tuxedos and pleated shirtfronts moved unobtrusively and attentively among the patrons. Even the busboys were carefully outfitted in turn-of-the-century butler coats with brass buttons that shone with a military glow on their chests.

Napped in pristine white, the lovely plain tables arranged around two rows of slim Corinthian columns in the large, open dining room were set with yellow daisies, vermeil flatware and little folded pyramids of napkins. Overhead, a thicket of crystal chandeliers bathed the room in just enough light to allow full appreciation of the cuisine's color and taste. Lazily swirling ceiling fans stirred the air, riffling the fronds of the potted palms and just perceptibly dulling the low hum of conversation.

Annie became aware that a man and two women several tables away were smiling and saying hello, while another woman, quite beautiful, nodded to Jake with more reserve. The latter woman, a striking brunette who slightly resembled Yolande Carr, was dining with an elderly gentleman. She regarded Annie with covert and distinctly envious curiosity.

Sitting there beneath portraits that he told her depicted the restaurant's founder and various members of his family, Jake looked more like a French Creole gentleman than ever. To her, he seemed totally at home in that environment where food and wine were meant to be taken seriously, yet where a certain sophisticated nonchalance would be greatly respected too, she guessed.

The little lines about his mouth curved with pleasure

as the menu was presented to him with a flourish, as if it were a papyrus scroll of great import being handed to a Roman senator.

"Smile, Annie," he prompted, with no trace of the unresolved issues between them apparent now in his beautiful eyes. "This is an elaborate and delightful game. It's best to take things lightheartedly, enjoy the specialness.

"The service may be impeccable, but there's no snobbery here. There aren't even any bread-and-butter plates. In the Creole tradition, it's all right to make a mess and get bread crumbs on the tablecloth. If you don't, the waiter will just have to brush imaginary ones away."

At her request, he ordered for both of them, making a deal with her to trade tidbits when their meals arrived. Because they were lovers—one person, really, he added—they should share.

"That way, I can introduce you to as many exquisite tastes as possible," he said. "Tonight, you're to put yourself completely in my hands. I want you to sit back and simply bask in being catered to."

In fact, Jake's topic for the evening seemed to be the pleasures of life as it was meant to be lived. As the wine was poured, he gave her a thumbnail history of the restaurant.

"It has quite a past," he said. "There are dining rooms upstairs that lock from the inside, to assure the utmost in privacy. It isn't hard to imagine how they might have been used during the city's nefarious past."

Their appetizers arrived—Oysters *Bienville* for their love life, Jake said—and Annie found that she was starving.

As the waiter refilled her glass with the heady white wine they had ordered, Jake tied his discourse about the restaurant to his central theme.

"Places like this are part of what makes life worth living," he said, raising his glass to her in an unspoken tribute. "Part of balancing pleasure with satisfying work, in a milieu where your roots go deep."

As the meal continued, he spoke more about balance —about his love for jazz on the one hand and his "respectable" career in architecture on the other; life in the city contrasted with what he had discovered with her in the bayou wilderness where she'd been raised.

"Now that I know the swamp and its beauty, I don't think I could be happy with an exclusively urban existence," he told her as he relished the last bite of his entree by mopping up the remaining sauce with a crusty bit of bread. "I'll want to go back again and again . . . find the peace you said drew you to return."

Halfway through their dinner, Jake had ordered a second bottle of wine. Her glass was automatically refilled as they talked and traded delicious morsels. By the time their plates had been cleared and coffee ordered, she felt quite relaxed, almost mesmerized by his words.

Gradually as they had dined and talked, the night had advanced around them, so that now the lights of the city shone through the frosted windowpanes beside their table with a festive glow. Meanwhile, the conversational hum from the other diners seemed to have escalated slightly. Despite that, she felt as if the two of them were on an island, alone together in a place no one else could reach.

"I've always felt balance to be important," he was telling her in a deep, quiet voice, taking both her hands in his across the table. "But I forget sometimes how you have to get your priorities straight to achieve it . . . do what means most to you but keep the other important things in your life as well.

"Like most people, I guess, I'm capable of holding back from change, all the risks it entails. Before you came into my life, I thought I had a satisfactory compromise worked out. I had loved and lost; ergo, I wouldn't let myself go with anyone I'd mind losing very much. In the interest of safety, I had condemned myself to a life without commitment, one that lacked the very decided pleasures of loving . . ."

His train of thought was interrupted as their waiter approached with a cart topped by a copper brazier and a minor forest of liquor bottles. "The owner sends his compliments, and hopes that M'sieur St. Arnold and the beautiful Mad'moiselle Duprez will enjoy sampling *café brûlot*," the waiter informed them. "You see, he has heard Mad'moiselle Duprez sing, and enjoyed it very much. He told me to add that he also enjoys watching people who are in love."

Smiling his lopsided smile, Jake gave a little salute of thanks to the restaurant owner, who was beaming at them from across the room. Preparation of the exotic coffee scented with orange and spice and liquor turned out to be quite a show. Heads turned as the brazier was lighted and the contents of the various bottles—Grand Marnier, rum, *crème de banane*, brandy—were blended with chicory-dark coffee from a silver pot.

Then a clove-studded orange was peeled in a corkscrew spiral, and the coffee mixture ignited. Deftly the waiter spooned the liquid over the orange, setting it momentarily alight in a waterfall of blue flame.

"That removes the acid from the orange peel," Jake whispered in response to her fascinated stare.

The coffee, served in a demitasse cup with a cavalier insignia, was delicious. "I never realized coffee could go to my head this way," Annie admitted, finishing her second tiny cup.

"As I'm certain my good friend, the owner of this establishment, intended that it should." Smiling at her, Jake ran one bluntly manicured finger around the rim of his own cup. The gesture was studied and sensual, as if he would have preferred to reach over and trace her cheek. "If you're finished, why don't we get out of here?" he suggested abruptly, edging his cup aside. "I want to go somewhere I can kiss you."

After settling up the bill, with a generous tip included, he helped her on with her jacket. Outside, the fresh air hit her with force, making her feel more unsteady than she had expected.

"You're tipsy," Jake noted with delight, putting one arm fully around her. "C'mon, sweetheart . . . a night-time stroll will do you good. I want to kiss you on the Moon Walk, overlooking the river. With Dabney underfoot, we never did finish our business there."

As they walked the seven short blocks from Arnaud's to Jackson Square, Jake nibbled at her ear and teased her outrageously, so that she was laughing and quite uninhibited by the time they were climbing the Moon Walk steps. Before them in the fitful moonlight, the broad river rolled past the old brewery on their right and lapped at a steamboat all lit up at its landing.

"You can't evade me now, Annie," Jake said lovingly, taking her into his arms and brushing against her mouth with his. "Now that I have you in a weakened condition, I'm going to make you listen—and insist on an answer."

"Oh, no," she parried, not catching his underlying seriousness yet. "It isn't fair . . . that restaurant owner was on your side."

In response, he enfolded her even more closely against him. "I imagine he was," he conceded. "I go in there quite often. But that's the first time he's ever seen me in love."

Undeniably, his words struck a responsive chord. But she wouldn't give over fencing with him yet. "Well, I'm not exactly unmoved in your company," she responded, slipping her arms around his neck.

"That won't do, Annie." There was an unaccustomed note of authority in his voice, a certain firmness in the strong grip of his hands. "You've confessed that you love me . . . when we're in bed together, and I'm making love to you. Say it now . . . standing here in a public place. Say that you'll mean it all our lives."

At last the magnitude of what he was asking began to penetrate. But it's true, she thought hazily. I'll always love Jake, no matter what the future may hold.

"Yes, darling," she responded, looking up at him with parted lips and wide gray eyes. "I'll love you forever."

"Ah, Annie . . ." His voice gruff with emotion, he laid his cheek against her hair. "Do you understand what that means? Sweetheart, I won't mind if you need to pursue your career single-mindedly for the next few years. As I started to tell you before, having you has made all the difference in my life. I understand now that I can dare to love you and that the child we'll make together someday won't steal Jamie's place. Once we're married and I know I have you, I won't find it so hard to wait—"

"Married?" Drawing back a little, she looked up at him in acute distress. "Is that what you're asking . . . for me to marry you?"

Something, a certain wariness perhaps, flickered in his eyes. "You've known all day long that's what I was asking," he said.

"Oh, Jake . . ." She turned her face away. All the old doubts and unhappiness were crowding back into her heart. Her quest to learn her mother's past had failed, even more miserably than if she'd found out nothing at all, and now she was facing the crisis she'd feared.

Maybe Solange didn't abandon me as I originally thought, she reasoned as clearly as she could. *She took me away with her when it became a choice between marriage and her career. But that's just what Jamie's mother felt she had to do.*

Loving Jake though she did, she felt the painful weight of her inheritance terribly in that moment. *I'm my mother's daughter,* she reminded herself bleakly, *and I can't risk hurting him even more*—though to lose him would almost be to die.

Handsome and dear and silent, he was waiting for her answer.

"I'm sorry, Jake," she whispered finally, her voice so low that he had to stoop a little to catch it. "I want you to know that I wasn't lying before when I said I love you. But there isn't any way that I can marry you."

11

Annie and Jake were two very silent, very unhappy people as they let themselves back into Jake's apartment. All the arguments that were likely to be proposed that night had already been offered as they'd faced each other on the Moon Walk, ironically one of New Orleans' most famous trysting spots.

Understandably, Jake had demanded she give him a reason to back up her categorical refusal of his proposal. But when she'd tried to make sense of what was a firmly held if irrational conviction, he was unable to understand. Instead, he muttered angrily at her when she insisted, on the verge of tears, that she was like her mother, a person not to be entrusted with his most precious hopes and dreams.

"You were right in the beginning to avoid me," she whispered, longing to take him in her arms but determinedly holding herself apart. "I've always known I was like her, though I tried to pretend otherwise . . . even to myself. You don't need another Laurelle to build your life around, only to find it empty again."

"Leave Jamie's mother out of it!" Furiously grinding out the words, he lit a cigarette and then just as quickly tossed it aside. "Don't you realize that you're nothing like her?" he demanded roughly. "And nothing like your own mother either, unless I miss my guess. Who put these ideas into your head, anyway? Your father? Somehow, I had a different impression of him than that."

"It wasn't Ned." At that point, her voice was nearly devoid of expression. "Nobody had to tell me, Jake."

Jake's hands, lacking the comfort of the cigarette, remained fiercely clenched at his sides. "Maybe you'd like to explain what it is you'd do to ruin my life if you married me," he suggested in a dangerous tone.

Feeling a little foolish, she tried to tell him how, someday, a spectacular singing job might come up in New York, one that she couldn't afford to turn down. Scarcely believing it herself, she described how she might have to leave him.

"How can you love me and say that?" he countered, the disbelief in his eyes mirroring her own.

Miserably, she shook her head. "It's *because* I love you that I don't want to risk hurting you. Solange didn't just walk away from Ned. Harold Dorsey, the man who used to run the club . . ." She paused. "He told me she was . . . promiscuous."

Jake swore again. *"And you think you're like that too?"*

She didn't answer, and for a long moment he also remained silent. "I don't think you'd leave me, Annie," he said finally, "not even if you believe it yourself. I know you too well now for that. And you should know me . . . realize that I'd *want* you to travel if that was important to you, as long as you always came home. As for that idiocy about you being promiscuous . . . well, that's exactly what it is. How could an angel like you be a tramp? And that's what you are, Annie . . . an angel. I know it whenever I hold you in my arms."

His words echoed in memory now in his apartment as he fixed himself a drink and lit another cigarette, this time to smoke it as thoroughly as if it would be his last. Uncertain, she stood there watching him, wondering what she should do. Most of her things were upstairs in his closet; during the past several weeks, his home had gradually become hers as well. Was she to go upstairs to bed with him then? she asked herself. Did he expect them to sleep awkwardly together like some married couple who'd just had a quarrel?

"Maybe I should go back to Sally's, at least for tonight," she proposed into the silence.

"No." His response was instantaneous, though he didn't quite look at her. "I don't want you to go."

That night, Annie wasn't surprised that they didn't make love. Feeling self-conscious for the first time without a nightgown, she donned one of his old shirts. Noting it without comment, he turned out the light and kissed her, then apparently went to sleep.

Oh, Jake, she thought, lying wakeful in the dark beside him. Don't you know how much I want to be the kind of person you think I am? How quickly I'd leap at what you're proposing if I were certain it could last?

Though his dark head rested on the pillow beside hers, she knew she couldn't expect an answer. In the scheme of things, that would have to come from her. Maybe I'm wrong, she thought, for the first time daring to consider the loving possibilities he had laid at her feet. Maybe I've allowed myself to become too obsessed with Solange and her mistakes simply because she's always been such an unknown quantity in my life.

In the morning, Jake cleared out early for an appointment at his office. For her part, Annie put in some required time at the oyster bar, then returned to the club in midafternoon to practice with the substitute pianist who would be filling in until Oscar's return. The man, whom Jake had hired only the day before, didn't show. Sitting meditatively at the piano in his place, she hummed one of her father's Cajun laments under her breath.

"Hello, Annie," someone said.

She glanced up at the greeting. "Harry!" she exclaimed in surprise. "I haven't seen you for ages."

He grinned. "I've been on assignment . . . and spending a lot of time with a girl from the investigative reporting staff, I might add."

"But that's wonderful."

Harry caught the off note in her voice. "How are things with you and Jake?" he countered in that direct way of his.

She shrugged, made a little face. "Unsettled at the moment, I guess. We were getting much too serious. I . . . think maybe I could handle that if I could settle some other things . . . like what my mother was really like, what kind of influence she was. But it doesn't look like that's ever going to happen."

To her surprise, Harry positively beamed. He sat down on the piano bench beside her. "On the contrary, I have some good news for you," he said. "We've found Marie Arnogne at last."

For a moment, Annie was speechless. "You've found her?" she repeated stupidly. Was it to be as simple as that, then? She took hold of his arms in her excitement. "Where is she, Harry?" she demanded, the questions tumbling over each other in her eagerness. "Does she remember my mother? Will she talk to me?"

"Hold on." Behind his owlish glasses, Harry's hazel eyes were alight. "In answer to your first question, she's in a nursing home . . . the Anderson Arms, in Gretna. Actually, my new friend found her while she was working on a story. Jennifer . . . that's my reporter friend . . . says Mrs. Arnogne has agreed to talk to you."

"Oh, Harry!" Overjoyed that his news had come just when she'd needed it most, she threw her arms around him, placed a big kiss on his cheek. "You're wonderful," she added. "I owe you so much."

Neither she nor Harry were aware that Jake had come into the courtyard looking for her, just in time to catch the little vignette.

Nor did they see the tight, angry look that settled on his face.

"I expect Jake's at the office," Harry said as she drew back to smile at him. "You can use my car if you want to go over this afternoon. Jenny's picking me up here in a few minutes anyway. Just park it in my spot out back when you return."

Jake's car was absent from its parking spot as she got behind the wheel of Harry's low-slung convertible. She had an almost fatalistic feeling as she backed out onto St. Peter Street and headed for the expressway. Whatever would be, would be.

But by the time she was approaching the bridge, Annie was brimming with mixed emotions. In perhaps half an hour she would be face-to-face with Marie Arnogne, whom she'd lost all hope of ever finding. Now that Harry *had* found her, she would have to hear whatever the woman had to say.

Maybe her memory won't be clear, she warned herself. But if it is, she might tell you the same thing Harold Dorsey did. What is it, anyway, that you wish you could hear?

Crossing the center span of the Mississippi River Bridge, the truth hit her in a little rush. More than anything in the world, she wanted her mother's landlady to tell her that everyone had been wrong about Solange—that the beautiful runaway singer had been anything but a tramp. I want to hear that she was a loving parent, she thought. And a misunderstood wife who'd been forced to make an unfair choice. I want Mrs. Arnogne to clear *my* name along with my mother's, give me permission to live the life I want.

In her heart, there wasn't any denying it. Though she had no intention of giving up her career, the life she wanted was with Jake.

There was a lump in Annie's throat as she parked the car in the shade of a spreading oak before the low brick building of the Anderson Arms. Here goes nothing, she thought, afraid and a little sick as she got out and walked up to the double glass front doors. All your hopes and all your despair.

To her surprise, the receptionist seemed to be expecting her. "My, yes, Miss Arnogne's been talkin' about nothin' else," she enthused. "The daughter of her old friend, comin' to see her after all these years."

The word *friend* stuck in Annie's mind as she followed the woman down a long tiled hallway to what was described as "Miss Arnogne's quad," a bed and sitting room shared by four elderly women in varying states of health.

"That's the lady you came to see," the woman informed her, nodding her head at a thin, fragile-looking old woman with distinctively Gallic features who was sitting propped by pillows in an upholstered lounger by the windows. "Go ahead. She's expectin' you."

Annie took one step and then another. Marie Arnogne glanced up, and a look of recognition lit her faded, watery eyes.

"Oh . . . oh, it's *you,*" the elderly woman quavered, holding out her hands. "You're so like your *maman.* I'd have known you anywhere. Please . . . please, come and sit down. I have the best chair; I apologize."

Like a sleepwalker, Annie moved forward to take Mrs. Arnogne's hands in hers. Fragile-looking and blue-veined, they were surprisingly strong.

"Thank you," said Annie hesitantly, "for letting me come to see you."

"Ah, but why not?" With a gently rueful smile, the old woman shook her head. "Little Annie . . . that's how I remember you . . . small and chubby, with fine, soft blond hair like an angel. You lighten it now—*non?* —the way your mother did. And you're every bit as beautiful."

There was no doubt that her mother's former land-lady was lucid, if more than a bit sentimental. Again she waved Annie to a seat in the straight-backed visitor's chair that had been placed beside her own, and this time Annie obeyed. "Was I . . . did I live with my mother at the Oakleaf then?" she asked.

"For a few months . . . until your father came to take you away." A shadow crossed the old woman's face as she confirmed that part of Harold Dorsey's story. "It happened while your mother was working," she added. "Your father arrived with a policeman, and a piece of paper given to him by the courts. Later, I had to tell her what had happened."

It wasn't hard to guess from Marie Arnogne's suddenly bleak tone how distraught and defenseless her mother had been. She could picture the landlady taking the slim, heartbroken singer in her arms, vainly trying to comfort her.

"Did she . . . miss me?" Annie asked, feeling like a fool but needing desperately to know. "I realize that's a stupid question. But I never saw her afterward. I don't even remember . . ."

"Pauvre p'tite." Sympathetically Marie Arnogne patted her hand. "It can't be any great comfort after all this time, but your mother was devoted to you. Except for her music, you were her life. It broke her heart when your father took you away."

"Then . . . why didn't she come after me?"

"I don't think she could. Your father had received something called a judgment. Anyway, that was long ago. I don't imagine the court looked kindly on her profession, or the fact that your father was essentially a decent man and she had left him of her own free will."

Annie shut her eyes tightly at the words, remembering Harold Dorsey's cutting indictment, *"a different man every night."*

"It was the men, wasn't it?" she asked in strangled tones. "They were the reason she couldn't fight him . . . and the reason he wouldn't leave me with her."

Marie Arnogne was frowning. "The men? But I don't understand. As far as I knew, she and your father were never really divorced. And there weren't any other men in her life . . . for the short time that it lasted."

"Harold Dorsey said—"

"Dorsey? That ruffian who ran the club where she sang?" Visibly, the old woman quelled a little upsurge of anger. "Tell me, Annie . . . what was it that Dorsey told you?"

For a moment, Annie didn't reply. "He said she was a tramp," she finally whispered. "A woman who had a new man every night. I . . . didn't want to believe him. But I couldn't find anybody else who remembered her."

Tears streaming down her cheeks, Annie bent her head. A moment later, Marie Arnogne was leaning forward, stroking her hair as if she were still the toddler the old woman remembered.

"There, *p'tite,* don't cry," she soothed. "There are names for people like that man. But we are ladies, *n'est-ce pas?* We don't descend to his level. Let me tell you the truth about how things stood. Your fine Mr. Dorsey had a bone to pick with Solange; though she worked in his club, she wouldn't let him spoil her virtue."

Pushing aside the faint hope that was rising, Annie shook her head. "So he invented these men, many years after the fact, just to carry out a grudge? I'm sorry. But I don't believe that."

"*Alors,* he didn't invent them. Your mother was a beautiful woman; in many ways, you are the image of her. Men flocked around Solange whenever she sang. And she was woman enough to enjoy the admiration. But she didn't take up with any of them, not even after you'd gone—though she told me that was what Ned expected her to do. 'I'm still a married woman, Marie,' she'd say. 'Even if my husband thinks I'm no better than a whore.' I used to feel that she planned to go home someday, after she was a big success, try to make him understand what she'd tried to do."

For several minutes the two of them sat there in silence, her mother's landlady reliving a scene more than two decades past, Annie trying to imagine it for the first time, with Marie Arnogne as her guide.

Finally Annie looked up, met the faded, compassionate eyes of her mother's friend. "And then she got sick," Annie said, her voice shaking a little on the words.

"Yes." There was a faraway look in the elderly woman's eyes. "I kept her on at the boardinghouse as long as I could. After a while, though, her illness became too pronounced, and I wasn't able to care for her. She wouldn't let me call your father . . . or her family in Vacherie. So she went to a place the city provided. I visited her there a few times before she died."

The utter sadness of Solange's end brought more tears, to be shared by the two of them as they sat close beside each other in the slanting late-afternoon sunlight. But there were happier memories, too, as Marie Arnogne described the specialness of the young singer she had befriended, her talent, and her love for the child she'd brought with her in the search for her dream.

"She had been spoiled as a child, I think," the landlady said. "And she was extremely impractical. But a sweeter, more loving soul I've never known."

It was nearly six when Annie tore herself away, full of affectionate thanks for the old woman's recollections, even those that had made her cry. Readily she promised to come again. "Perhaps we can take a walk in the garden next time," she suggested. "Or even a drive somewhere, if you're feeling up to that."

Marie Arnogne squeezed her hands tightly, as if she were reluctant to let them go. "You can't imagine how much I'd enjoy that, *chérie*," she said.

Returning to the city, Annie was rapt in thought. Harold Dorsey was wrong, she said to herself over and over again, repeating it like a litany. Despite his desire to get even, despite Ned's jealousy, my mother wasn't a woman of loose morals at all—certainly not a tramp who left her husband for the lure of other men. When the writer of that newspaper story said she had the rare quality of innocence, he wasn't mistaken.

Well, my mother might have loved me enough to take me with her, and to mourn my loss the way Marie Arnogne said, she acknowledged. And maybe she didn't leave my father with the intention of living a dissolute life. But leave him she did—and for her career, the same reason Jamie's mother left Jake.

There was no denying the truth of that accusation. Yet as Annie left the bridge and headed back toward the Quarter, she found herself in possession of a fresh insight: for Solange and Ned, the situation had been an impossible one.

Firmly planted in Houma and the swamp by his stubborn Cajun roots, Ned would have flatly refused to follow his wife to the city for anything so frivolous as a singing career. Solange, trapped there as Annie herself had felt trapped during her father's lifetime, would have been blocked from pursuing a jazz career in a town where waltzes and folk songs were the abiding rhythms, and the accordion and harmonica the most favored instruments.

When finally her need for expression had driven her away, Ned's jealousy hadn't allowed him to see the truth. My parents were at an impasse, she acknowledged. And it was *nobody's* fault. I know now that they both loved me, and even suspect that they loved each other, that it was like a kind of death for them to part. But their very natures collided, their most fervent dreams. There simply wasn't anything else they could do.

Joyously her inner self changed sides, arguing now for what deep in her heart she'd wanted from the first moment Jake had held her in his arms. The conflict between Solange and Ned doesn't have any meaning for you, it declared. Jake lives in New Orleans, not Houma, and jazz is part of his livelihood.

Only the night before, Jake had hinted he could come to love the swamp the way she did, could willingly share that part of herself. And he'd told her he would understand if she had to travel sometimes, provided she always came home to him.

You even want to have his child someday, Annie told herself sharply. What are you waiting for, an avalanche to hit you before you tell him yes?

By the time Annie pulled Harry's convertible into its parking spot, the Corvette was back in its customary place.

Is Jake upstairs? she wondered, suddenly bursting with the desire to tell him what she had learned. But then she remembered that the St. Petersburg drawings were finished, and that he wouldn't be closeted in the apartment now. Anyway, it was already twenty minutes to seven. Music drifted out into the courtyard. Some-body else was on the drums and they were still lacking a piano player. He would be inside the club as usual, she guessed, keeping an eye on things.

But he wasn't at his regular table. A moment later, she spotted him at the bar, a Scotch in his hand and his back to the musicians. Beside him, a heavily made-up brunette was flirting, trying without success to get his attention.

What's wrong? she asked herself with an apprehensive feeling as she slid onto the empty stool on his opposite side. Has something happened to sabotage the Florida Centre project?

Jake's dark brows lifted a little at the sight of her. "Cheers," he said tersely, saluting her with his glass. "I didn't expect to see you here this evening."

She was a little taken aback. "But . . . why not?" she asked.

He shrugged. "I thought you and Harry might have gone somewhere together."

"Harry and I?" Her puzzlement deepened. "But I don't understand . . . Darling, I borrowed his car to go over to Gretna, to see Marie Arnogne. She's in a nursing home there. Harry found her for me."

For a moment his blue eyes lit with interest. Then, "I assume you were properly grateful," he said without much expression.

Annie laid one hand over his. "Of course I'm grateful," she said. "Don't you expect me to be? Jake, there's something else going on here, something you're not saying."

"Something *I'm* not saying?" He swore. "Don't try to make a fool of me, Annie. I saw the two of you earlier,

169

in each other's arms. But you don't have to remind me . . . you're a free agent, and you can be as grateful as you damn please . . . to anyone you choose."

For a moment she simply stared at him, trying to make sense of what he was saying. "You think . . . that Harry and I . . ." The words came out haltingly as she remembered the scene at the piano bench that afternoon. "You don't really believe that, do you?" she asked softly.

"Does it really matter?" He shoved his glass across at the bartender, signaling for another Scotch. "You made your point last night," he added, not quite looking at her. "Your mother was a tramp; therefore you must be one too. And you're bent on proving that, for God knows what crazy reason. Just don't expect me to hang around and watch, baby. That's all I ask."

Horrified at what he was saying, Annie could feel her temper rising, that stubborn Cajun temper she had inherited from Ned. "Maybe *I'm* the one who shouldn't hang around," she retorted ominously.

For the space of several seconds he didn't reply. "If you want to break your contract, there won't be any recriminations on my part," he said at last.

Not waiting for the drink he'd ordered, Jake got to his feet. With a little gesture of dismissal, he turned his back on her and went out the courtyard door.

Annie followed him with her eyes, a sick feeling washing over her. Yet by this time she was very angry indeed, angry enough not to cry. *All right,* she thought, hugging that anger to her as a perverse kind of comfort. Have it your way. There's no use insisting you listen to the truth. I can't have both a singing career and a man who isn't capable of trust.

She would get her things from his apartment later.

Carried on a wave of indignation, Annie stormed out of Paradise Lost. I hope Stephen Morel meant it when he said I could reconsider his offer to do the concert, she said to herself as she marched back to Sally's on foot. And about his connections. Because he's going to be hearing from me tonight.

12

Mercifully, when Annie got to Sally's apartment, Sally was nowhere about. With a mixture of relief and regret, Annie was able to reach Stephen Morel on the first try at his private number. He hadn't yet signed another singer for his concert.

"I'm absolutely delighted you've changed your mind," the wealthy developer said. "I don't suppose I could talk you into coming over to St. Pete a few weeks early? We'll need some time to put the program together, of course. But you might enjoy the change, and I can guarantee you a part-time singing job meanwhile. I have an interest in a little cabaret at Jannus Landing here."

With a heavy heart, she agreed to do as he asked. There were only two weeks to run in her contract, and Jake had said he wouldn't hold her to it anyway. What does it matter *when* I leave, she thought, if Jake wants me to go?

Clad only in her slip, Annie was curled miserably on her bed in the darkened apartment when, an hour later, someone began pounding at the door.

"Let me in," Jake pleaded, his deep voice rough with emotion. "I owe you an apology, sweetheart."

Dazed and a little hesitant, she opened the door.

"Harry came back to the club maybe twenty minutes ago . . . with his new lady love," he admitted contritely, taking her hands in his. "Somebody told him what had happened between us."

"And he set you straight?"

"In no uncertain terms. He's mad as hell at me . . ."

"So am I," she said, even while her love for him surfaced again. "So am I."

"You have every right to be, sweetheart. Every right to tell me no. But say you'll forgive me anyway and come back with me. I don't ever want you to go."

Annie shut her eyes tightly for a moment. "I'm afraid I can't help it," she confessed. "When you said . . . what you did about my contract . . . I called Stephen Morel. I've agreed to do his St. Petersburg concert at the end of the month."

Jake stared as her meaning registered. "You can change your mind back again," he said, trying to draw her into his arms.

Resisting him, she shook her head. "No," she said. "I can't do that. But I don't have to leave immediately, the way he asked me to. I can finish out the final two weeks of our contract. But then I have to go."

There was something implacable in her words that he couldn't mistake. "It isn't just that you gave your word," he asked after a moment, "is it?"

"No," she said. "It's not. You're right."

Don't you see? she added silently. Now I have to find out what happens if I do this. Find out whether or not our love can survive. That afternoon, after Mrs. Arnogne told her the truth about Solange, she had been ready to take a chance. But his jealousy had made her afraid again—of the way they might hurt each other.

Jake just stood there looking at her, as if he were trying to read her silence. "When's the concert?" he asked finally.

"Three weeks from Saturday."

"All right. Afterward, you're coming back to New Orleans."

"Maybe. I can't promise that yet."

Even in Bethia Jacobsen's gazebo, when he'd told her about his son, his face hadn't had such a bleak expression as it did now. "Come home with me now, then," he requested, quietly overcoming her objections and putting his arms around her. "At least you can stay with me until you have to go."

Their lovemaking that night was fierce and tender and so sad that Annie wanted to weep. Lying in his big bed with him afterward, she thought that, despite a shared physical release, their bodies had failed to achieve a unity their souls had lost. I don't know if I'm going to be able to go through with this, she admitted to herself. I love him too much to cause him pain. Still, she had to know the truth—to satisfy herself that they could make a life together.

Throughout the final two weeks of her contract at Paradise Lost, she and Jake were together in that unaccustomed way—inseparable but with a wall between them that neither could surmount. Oscar came home from the hospital, and on her final night at the club he was back at the ivories again.

"I heard what went down between you an' your man," he told her in that direct, down-to-earth way of his just before they started the evening's show. "You're makin' a big mistake. Ain't ever'body got what you two found."

Annie didn't try to explain, perhaps because she was no longer certain herself she understood. She and Jake had made love for what might have been the last time that afternoon, clinging together after it was over, then finally moving apart. Following her performance, Stephen Morel's private jet would be waiting at the airport to claim her.

Her heart was aching as she took the microphone, to romance it with the songs they both loved—the blues number he'd insisted she sing at her audition, the song that had been her vehicle the evening she had made love to him with her eyes.

Jake was at the drums, his tie loosened and his shirt sleeves rolled up to reveal his muscular forearms, pouring all the frustration and heartache he surely felt into his music. To the delight of the crowd, he did one virtuoso solo after another. Only Annie and perhaps Oscar and Harry understood the depth of his anger and sadness.

He must be unique in all the world, she thought as she watched him make the drums sputter and growl and roar. A man so special that nothing else should matter beside him. I'm a fool to risk losing him this way.

Yet by this time the matter seemed out of her hands. She felt carried forward by events and commitments, by her own uncertainty. Once in Florida, she knew, she'd be separated from him by more than physical distance. The fact that she could leave him at all without any promise to return would have to be reckoned with. Fears that she couldn't quite put into words would have to be confronted and laid to rest. Without his help, she would have to lift the weight of his jealousy from her heart.

They didn't talk very much later as they drove out to the airport. Quietly she laid her hand on his knee so that he could cover it with his own. But though she had maintained a surface calm, her heart lurched a little when she saw that Morel's Learjet was waiting. As they pulled up beside it, the developer's uniformed pilot emerged, ready to transfer her baggage.

"I suppose this is goodbye," said Jake, taking her in his arms. She could feel his love and longing surround her.

"Maybe not," she whispered. Tears glittered in her eyes as she raised her mouth to his. "Maybe it won't have to be the way it seems . . ."

"Annie, Annie . . . don't forget how much I love you." Roughly and yet with the greatest of tenderness, his mouth came down on hers to possess it with just a hint of desperation. She could feel his well-loved body pressing against her as if by the sheer physical force of his affection he could keep her at his side.

A moment later, he simply let her go. "Come back to me," he whispered, not as if he expected any response.

He was still standing there when they taxied out along the runway and lifted off into the night. Jake, she cried out to him in silent anguish, alone in the passenger cabin as the tears finally came. Without you, how much can a career matter?

Yet she was Ned Duprez's daughter as much as

Solange's. And she had made up her mind to find out, in the only way possible, what their future might hold.

At the St. Petersburg-Clearwater Airport, Morel himself was waiting. Greeting her with his usual warm politeness, he whisked her into his limousine—though not before he had noticed the puffiness about her eyes and shrewdly guessed its cause, she was certain.

As promised, she was treated like visiting royalty, put up in a guest suite that adjoined the wealthy developer's fourteenth-floor apartment, where she had access to his perfectly tuned Steinway. She had a private balcony of her own overlooking the yacht basin and the blue expanse of Tampa Bay. The limousine and driver were at her service whenever she needed them. Each night, including the several occasions on which she sang at his club, she dined with her host, either alone or in the company of his friends.

Though in effect she was living under his roof, Stephen Morel made no physical move in her direction. Unfailingly courteous, he limited most of their discussions to his business and her career, inquiring with interest about her aspirations.

When she was not rehearsing with the symphony for the concert or spending time with him, she wandered in a wilderness of the heart. On her balcony, basking in the warm Florida sunshine, she spent long hours staring at the vast panorama of water below, silvered with cross-currents in the sunlight. Without really seeing them, she let her gaze rest on the moored sailboats that, like winged steeds, waited motionless in their slips.

Outside her loneliness, people were biking, strolling or working on their boats, enjoying one another and the breeze that flickered through the palms around the sleepy waterfront. It's so beautiful here, she thought, like a picture postcard. And to me, just as unreal.

During the short time she'd sung at Paradise Lost, she had come to love the sometimes seamy, always cultivated city of New Orleans almost as much as she loved Jake. It had become home to her.

Wherever her career might take her—New York, Dallas, even the exhilarating and terrifying frontier of the West Coast—that place would lack the Crescent City's unique and rich ambiance, just as it would be empty of him. She would find herself longing for beignets and chicory-flavored coffee, she knew, the wild and colorful panorama of Bourbon Street, even while her soul ached for the comfort of his arms.

Lying there with the sun beating down on her oil-scented skin, she could think only of the man she loved, wondering what he was doing or feeling. She knew now that, without intending to, she'd become a one-man woman, and a one-city woman in the bargain. But she wasn't sure that she could go back to him even if she *were* willing to curtail her career. In the week since they had said goodbye, he hadn't written or called. Probably he's given up on me by this time, she thought unhappily. I wonder if he's been having his doubts about us too.

When, on the day of the concert, she finally called him, the phone rang in what was apparently an empty apartment. Harry wasn't at the club, and no one else there seemed to know Jake's whereabouts. Of course, she was too proud to call his uncle and aunt. And the architectural firm would definitely be closed for the weekend.

There's nothing I can do tonight, she thought, slipping on the white, paillette-encrusted dress Stephen Morel had bought her at one of the Beach Drive shops. Vigorously she brushed her hair into a slanting, silvery blond curtain, the way she'd worn it ever since Jake had arranged it that way. I'll have to give this my all tonight, go on with the show in the best show business tradition, she decided. Afterward, I've just got to get up the courage to go back and set things straight with Jake. I can't run away blindly from what I want most in the world.

While the dinner-on-the-ground segment of the huge Picnic n' Pops gathering in Straub Park was taking place, Stephen Morel carried her off to a private dinner with him at The Pier. Despite her insistence that she was never hungry before a performance, he'd reserved a windowside table at a seafood restaurant that hovered over the bay's milky blue water.

He didn't press her to eat. Instead, he ordered wine to relax her, then got directly to the point.

"You've probably wondered why I haven't . . . pressed myself on you, Annie," he said, folding his hands around the stem of his glass. "In my experience, a woman always senses a man's interest, so I don't doubt you're aware of how I feel about you."

Momentarily taken aback, she chose not to respond.

"Part of the reason is Jake St. Arnold, and the fact that I respect him," he continued, quite as if she'd spoken. "But it's more than that. I had hoped that, once you were here in St. Petersburg, you would forget him, see in me the sort of person who could advise and help you, gradually come to feel some affection. That hasn't happened, though."

"You're not entirely right," she said candidly, following his example. "I like you very much. But I might as well admit it: I love Jake with all my heart."

The developer regarded her quizzically for a moment. "Do you mind my asking what the problem is, then?"

Instinctively trusting her self-possessed host, Annie laid down the burden of her uncertainty and loneliness. In a low voice, she told him everything—the quest to find Solange's past and her own fears that she would repeat her mother's mistakes. With a quaver in her voice, she described her relief on learning the truth. She suffered only minor pangs of disloyalty at disclosing Jake's misplaced jealousy and his remorse.

"Jake and I . . . remained lovers right up until the night I left New Orleans," she admitted, meeting Stephen's eyes. "But after the incident with Harry, something went out of our relationship, something I didn't know how to replace. I don't want to live with jealousy, and I started to have some of the same fears I'd had before."

Sighing, Stephen shook his head. "Can't you see how it must appear to Jake, Annie?" he asked. "Imagine how he must feel, wondering what would have happened if you'd never found your mother's landlady, or learned the truth. If I were him, I'd want you to take the relationship on its own merits, not subordinate it to something that had happened to others, in the past."

Annie stared, confounded by the simplicity and clarity of his insight. "You're right," she said slowly. "Somehow I didn't see that before. He'd have every right to feel betrayed. But . . . what about his jealousy? Isn't that the same thing? He didn't acknowledge he was wrong about Harry and me until after Harry had made him face the truth. If we're to have any kind of chance together, he'd have to trust me more than that."

Stephen nodded. "I'm sure you're right. But it seems to me things might be different if he had your assurance you were playing for keeps." Pausing a moment to see whether she had absorbed his message, he set his napkin beside his plate and got to his feet. "Pardon me, but I've got a phone call to make," he said thoughtfully. "It shouldn't take too long. Will you be all right here alone?"

By the time it was dark and Annie was waiting in the wings of the improvised stage in Straub Park, she had made up her mind. If I have to hitchhike back to New Orleans when this concert is finished, she thought, then that's what I'm going to do. Stephen is right; we didn't show enough faith in each other. Whatever Jake and I have left to work out between us, it amounts to nothing in the face of a life without him.

Then she was being introduced. Applause filled the park as she walked out to the microphone to face the firefly glow of hundreds of lanterns pinpointing the concertgoers seated on blankets and lawn chairs in the dark. As she and the conductor had arranged, she began with several effervescent, upbeat numbers that drew a hearty response, then moved on to tackle a number of hard-driving forties classics in her most brassy and forthright style.

She was singing as well as she ever had, with the great, rich sound of the symphony behind her and certain crucial points settled in her heart at last. Meanwhile, the same old love affair with the audience unfolded, as demanding as ever, and she gloried in it now that her mind was at rest. I'm always going to need this magic too, she thought. But I absolutely refuse to give up the man I love to have it.

When she had pushed the fast-paced numbers as far as she could, she changed the pace, becoming at once sexy and misty and mellow. I chose the songs in this segment for Jake, she realized, shaking back her hair and using the line of her body the way he'd taught her. Even though he won't hear them tonight. I love you, darling, she promised him as she concluded her performance. I'm coming home to you.

The applause was thunderous as she left the stage, then returned for several bows and the conductor's congratulations. Then she was stepping back into the wings again, out of the public view.

"Someone's waiting to speak to you," Stephen Morel was saying as he gave her a hand down the makeshift steps.

She glanced about, expecting to see a reporter with a notepad or camera. And then she saw him. He was standing there in light-colored trousers and a dark polo shirt, just looking at her the way he had at the airport, his eyes compelling even in the dark.

"*Jake!*" The single word was wrung from her as she broke free of Stephen Morel's guiding hand and threw herself into his arms. "Darling," she said breathlessly, her heart racing, "I thought—"

"That I could stay away? Baby, I didn't want to. But I might have been fool enough if it hadn't been for the best client I'll ever have."

"Stephen?"

He nodded, giving the developer a little salute. The next moment he was catching her hand in a crushing grip. "C'mon," he said, dragging her away through the crowd. "I've been missing you like hell. Let's get out of here."

Stunned at his presence, she didn't ask where they were going. Behind them, the first notes of the Tchaikovsky overture were filling the night as he propelled her along, so swiftly that she almost had to run to stay beside him.

They had gone several blocks that way when one of her spike heels nearly caught and turned on a broken place in the pavement. "Jake, please!" she cried. "I can't run. Not in this dress, and with these shoes!"

Her words stopped him, and he pulled her tightly against him. "I can carry you if you like, angel," he said after a moment, the little lines beside his mouth curving as he looked down at her. "Even if we're already at our destination."

"Stephen's apartment?"

He nodded, suddenly smiling his wicked smile. "He called me tonight—while the two of you were having dinner, I understand—and told me to get myself out to the airport. It just so happened his company jet was in the neighborhood. I made it in time for your final number."

They were standing outside the lavish apartment building's lobby entrance, and the concierge, in his glass enclosure, had noticed them. "I asked if you wanted me to carry you," Jake reminded, glancing at the uniformed guard and then back at her.

"I'd absolutely adore it," Annie replied, all her love for him showing in her eyes.

Scooping her up, he opened the door as handily as if it were an everyday occurrence.

"Good evening," Annie told the concierge with exaggerated politeness as Jake carried her into the mural-paneled elevator and pressed the button.

He was kissing her as they zoomed upward, with the result that they almost neglected to get out before the door closed again on the fourteenth-floor corridor. "Sweetheart, I don't have a key," she remembered. "What are we going to do?"

With a grin, Jake produced a small brass key and fitted it into the lock, shoving the massive front door open with his foot. "Morel gave it to me himself," he explained, "along with the injunction that, if I didn't make good use of it, I deserved to lose you."

Seconds later, he had set her on her feet and she was in his arms. Immediately she knew that, whatever they had been lacking before, it had been returned to them. As if a match had been put to dry tinder, their loving banter was blazing up into passion.

"Morel gave me two hours," Jake murmured, his hands pushing down the bodice of her dress. "Not much time for the kind of love I want to make with you."

"Not nearly enough. Oh, Jake . . . I want you over and over again . . . twice, no *three* times for every lovemaking that we've lost."

A moment later they had gone beyond words. They undressed each other with loving haste in Morel's dining room, draping their things over his priceless Queen Anne chairs or just letting them drop to the carpet. Then Jake was drawing her to the living area's magnificent wall of glass, just as the fireworks that accompanied the overture's traditional cannon shots lit the night sky.

Overhead was a bright galleon moon. The cheers of

the crowd, the stirring chords of the music, carried to them faintly on the air.

"I want you here by the window," Jake whispered, his hands caressing her breasts, smoothing the satiny skin of her shoulders. "So I can see your beautiful body without turning on the lights."

Arranging several oversized throw pillows for her head, he made her lie back while he traced a fiery path of kisses from her mouth to the very core of her desire. How I've needed him, she thought, even as she was swept upward in a spiral of ever-mounting rapture. If I live to be a hundred, I'll never dream of really leaving him again.

In what seemed only moments, she was moaning and shuddering beneath his caresses. Then he was covering her with his body, plunging within to bring her back to the heights again, heights they climbed together in a soaring, rapturous union.

The last of the concert crowd was dispersing below when, later, they lay spent against the pillows. "Marry me," Jake said softly, tracing her profile with one finger. "Trust that I won't be fool enough to lose you again."

Still overwhelmed with his love, Annie felt her response catch in her throat, so thankful was she for the chance to give it. "Yes, Jake," she agreed. "I'll marry you."

He was silent a moment. "Just like that?" he asked. "No bargains to be struck?"

"No bargains. We've been through all that before. I know everything I need to know."

For a moment she thought he would make love to her again on the spot, so fierce was his pleasure in her answer. But then he got up and walked to the dining room again, rummaged about in his pockets.

She was certain when he returned to her and flicked on his lighter that all he'd wanted was a cigarette. But by the light of the flame she saw that he was handing her a small velvet box. She opened it with trembling fingers.

"Oh, Jake," she exclaimed, drawing forth a ring that caught and swirled little pivot points of light. "It's so beautiful . . ."

"Hold out your hand, sweetheart." With exquisite care he slipped the circlet of emeralds and diamonds on her finger. "I had it in my pocket that night on the Moon Walk," he told her. "Do you know what it's meant to represent?"

Lost in her love for him, Annie couldn't begin to guess.

"Duckweed," he supplied, looking inordinately pleased with himself. "The little emeralds are the leaves, and the diamonds, water droplets. There's a paper that goes with it . . ."

"Not a marriage license?"

"In a way." He unfolded an official-looking document, then held his lighter up again so that she could read.

"Ned's trapping lease . . ." Annie stared up at him in amazement. "But this says it's transferred to Annie and Jake St. Arnold."

"I didn't want it to pass out of the family." His blue eyes were gleaming at her there in the dark. "Maybe someday . . ."

Filled with images of what they would share someday, she burrowed against him. "When our children are old enough . . .," she prompted.

186

"We'll take them there." Jake's voice was rough with emotion. "In the meantime . . ."

"It's an absolutely marvelous place for us to be together."

There would be time enough later to explain how carefully she would make certain never to abuse the freedom he had so lovingly accorded while offering her his name and his heart.

Time enough to assure him how much she would treasure the little duckweed ring and the curious meld of city streets and bayou refuge that would be their lives.

Just now, the two hours Stephen Morel had granted them were on the wing. "Make love to me again," she whispered softly, slipping her arms about his neck. "I want to be thoroughly yours when we fly back to New Orleans tonight."

ANNOUNCING:

WIN

$50,000

DIAMOND JEWELRY COLLECTION

OR

ONE OF 100 ONE-YEAR BOOK CLUB SUBSCRIPTIONS TO THE SILHOUETTE SERIES OF YOUR CHOICE

Look for the ◇ **on all Silhouette Romance, Special Edition, Desire and Intimate Moments starting with June publications.**

SDS-A-1

If you've enjoyed this book, mail this coupon and get 4 thrilling

Silhouette Desire®

novels FREE (a $7.80 value)

If you've enjoyed this Silhouette Desire novel, you'll love the 4 __FREE__ books waiting for you! They're yours as our gift to introduce you to our home subscription service.

**Get Silhouette Desire novels
before they're available anywhere else.**

Through our home subscription service, you can get Silhouette Desire romance novels regularly—delivered right to your door! Your books will be *shipped to you two months before they're available anywhere else*—so you'll never miss a new title. Each month we'll send you 6 new books to look over for 15 days, without obligation. If not delighted, simply return them and owe nothing. Or keep them and pay only $1.95 each. There's no charge for postage or handling. And there's no obligation to buy anything at any time. You'll also receive a subscription to the Silhouette Books Newsletter *absolutely free!*

So don't wait. To receive your four FREE books, fill out and mail the coupon below *today!*

SILHOUETTE DESIRE and colophon are registered trademarks and a service mark.

Silhouette Desire® 120 Brighton Road, P.O. Box 5084, Clifton, N.J. 07015-5084

Yes, please send me FREE and without obligation, 4 exciting Silhouette Desire books. Unless you hear from me after I receive them, send me 6 new Silhouette Desire books to preview each month before they're available anywhere else. I understand that you will bill me just $1.95 each for a total of $11.70—with no additional shipping, handling or other hidden charges. **There is no minimum number of books that I must buy, and I can cancel anytime I wish.** The first 4 books are mine to keep, even if I never take a single additional book.

☐ Mrs. ☐ Miss ☐ Ms. ☐ Mr.   BDD2H5

Name _____ *(please print)*

Address _____ Apt. # _____

City _____ State _____ Zip _____
( )
Area Code   Telephone Number

Signature (If under 18, parent or guardian must sign.)

This offer, limited to one per customer. Terms and prices subject to change. Your enrollment is subject to acceptance by Silhouette Books.

DD-R-A

An epic novel of exotic rituals
and the lure of the Upper Amazon

THE TAKERS RIVER OF GOLD

JERRY AND S.A. AHERN

THE TAKERS are the intrepid Josh Culhane and the seductive Mary Mulrooney. These two adventurers launch an incredible journey into the Brazilian rain forest. Far upriver, the jungle yields its deepest secret—the lost city of the Amazon warrior women!

THE TAKERS series is making publishing history. Awarded *The Romantic Times* first prize for High Adventure in 1984, the opening book in the series was hailed by *The Romantic Times* as "the next trend in romance writing and reading. Highly recommended!"

Jerry and S.A. Ahern have never been better!

TAK–3

A Gold Eagle book from Worldwide, available now wherever Harlequin and Silhouette paperbacks are sold

For the woman who expects a little more out of love, get Silhouette Special Edition.

Take 4 books free—no strings attached.

If you yearn to experience more passion and pleasure in your romance reading ... to share even the most private moments of romance and sensual love between spirited heroines and their ardent lovers, then Silhouette Special Edition has everything you've been looking for.

Get 6 books each month before they are available anywhere else!

Act now and we'll send you four exciting Silhouette Special Edition romance novels. They're our gift to introduce you to our convenient home subscription service. Every month, we'll send you six new passion-filled Special Edition books. Look them over for 15 days. If you keep them, pay just $11.70 for all six. Or return them at no charge.

We'll mail your books to you *two full months before they are available* anywhere else. Plus, with every shipment, you'll receive the Silhouette Books Newsletter absolutely free. *And with Silhouette Special Edition there are never any shipping or handling charges.*

Mail the coupon today to get your four free books — and more romance than you ever bargained for.

Silhouette Special Edition is a service mark and a registered trademark.

── MAIL COUPON TODAY ──

Silhouette Special Edition®
120 Brighton Road, P.O. Box 5084, Clifton, N.J. 07015-5084

☐ Yes, please send me FREE and without obligation, 4 exciting Silhouette Special Edition romance novels. Unless you hear from me after I receive my 4 FREE BOOKS, please send me 6 new books to preview each month. I understand that you will bill me just $1.95 each for a total of $11.70 — with no additional shipping, handling or other charges. **There is no minimum number of books that I must buy, and I can cancel anytime I wish.** The first 4 books are mine to keep, even if I never take a single additional book.

BSD2R5

☐ Mrs.   ☐ Miss   ☐ Ms.   ☐ Mr.

Name _____ (please print)

Address _____ Apt. No. _____

City _____ State _____ Zip _____

Signature (If under 18, parent or guardian must sign.)

This offer, limited to one per customer. Terms and prices subject to change. Your enrollment is subject to acceptance by Silhouette Books.

SE-OP-A

Enjoy romance and passion, larger-than-life...

Now, thrill to 4 Silhouette Intimate Moments novels (a $9.00 value)— ABSOLUTELY FREE!

If you want more passionate sensual romance, then Silhouette Intimate Moments novels are for you!

In every 256-page book, you'll find romance that's electrifying...involving... and intense. And now, these larger-than-life romances can come into your home every month!

4 FREE books as your introduction.

Act now and we'll send you four thrilling Silhouette Intimate Moments novels. They're our gift to introduce you to our convenient home subscription service. Every month, we'll send you four new Silhouette Intimate Moments books. Look them over for 15 days. If you keep them, pay just $9.00 for all four. Or return them at no charge.

We'll mail your books to you *as soon as they are published.* Plus, with every shipment, you'll receive the Silhouette Books Newsletter absolutely free. *And Silhouette Intimate Moments is delivered free.*

Mail the coupon today and start receiving Silhouette Intimate Moments. Romance novels for women...not girls.

Silhouette Intimate Moments

Silhouette Intimate Moments™
120 Brighton Road, P.O. Box 5084, Clifton, N.J. 07015-5084

☐ YES! Please send me FREE and without obligation, 4 exciting Silhouette Intimate Moments romance novels. Unless you hear from me after I receive my 4 FREE books, please send 4 new Silhouette Intimate Moments novels to preview each month. I understand that you will bill me $2.25 each for a total of $9.00 — with no additional shipping, handling or other charges. **There is no minimum number of books to buy and I may cancel anytime I wish.** The first 4 books are mine to keep, even if I never take a single additional book.

☐ Mrs. ☐ Miss ☐ Ms. ☐ Mr.   BMD225

Name _____ (please print) _____

Address _____ Apt. # _____

City _____ State _____ Zip _____
(   )
Area Code   Telephone Number

Signature (if under 18, parent or guardian must sign)

This offer, limited to one per customer. Terms and prices subject to change. Your enrollment is subject to acceptance by Silhouette Books.

SILHOUETTE INSPIRATIONS is a trademark and service mark

IM-OP-A